DISASTER
IN HIS WAKE

The Strange Life of Horatio Evans

Book One

Ray Noyes

WORDCATCHER publishing

The Strange Life of Horatio Evans: Book One
Disaster in His Wake

© 2015-17 Ray Noyes
Illustrations © Picasso Griffiths

The Author asserts the moral right to be identified as the author of this work. All rights reserved.

This book is protected under the copyright laws of the United Kingdom. Any reproduction or other unauthorised use of the material herein is prohibited without the express written permission of the Publisher.

British Library Cataloguing in Publication Data.
A catalogue record for this book is available from the British Library.

Second Edition, 2017
Paperback ISBN: 9781912056408

First published under the title *Abertwp Awakes – Horatio Evans, Communist and Welsh Nutter Wreaks Havoc* by Y Lolfa Cyf, 2015.

Edited and re-published by Wordcatcher Publishing.

www.wordcatcher.com
facebook.com/WordcatcherPublishing

Category: Humour / Politics

Dedicated with love to Horatio's descendants.

Only two characters are based on real persons, Horatio and Gladys Evans. All other characters are fictitious and any resemblance to persons living or dead is purely coincidental and unintended.

A hero is born in a 1,000,
A wise man is found in 10,000,
Fools are everywhere.

After Plato

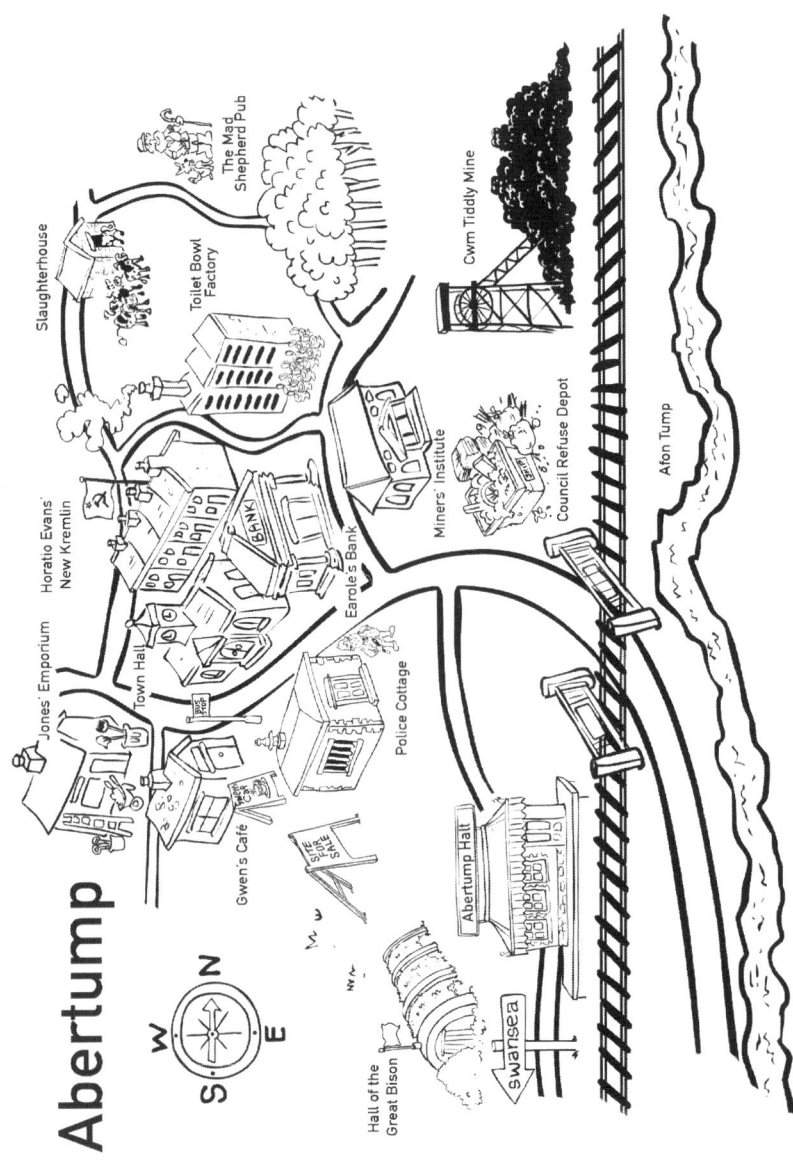

Contents

Preface	i
A Hero is Born	1
His Formative Years	11
Taking the Wheel	25
Councillor Horatio Evans	41
The Conservatory	49
The Wardrobe	79
The Fireplace	101
The Kind Kangaroo	119
The Horticultural Adventure	145
No Surrender	165

PREFACE

This is the first in a series of four books charting the crazy adventures and even crazier dreams of one Horatio ap Llewelyn Evans: councillor, amateur communist, father of two and husband of the long-suffering and mysteriously ill Gladys. The stories are set in a small, fictitious mining town in the Swansea Valley where all was peaceful and relatively contented until he arrived. Most of its voters seemed satisfied with their lot, whether working down the mines, in the toilet bowl factory or the slaughterhouse, but they were to be shaken out of their complacency by someone who thought it about time that the capitalist system beneath which they toiled was confronted head on. Horatio Evans had arrived.

This first volume is an introduction to the man: his birth and development and eventually his strange and disruptive effect upon the lovely town. We get to know him as he focuses his attention and energy on crazy attempts at improving his home using his unique communist-inspired approach to DIY; but once achieved, he set his sights on grander schemes, some so grand as to be beyond the imaginings of most mortals – certainly any in Abertump. These grand schemes are the subjects of further books in the series.

In case the reader infers that these stories are entirely fictitious, he should ignore such a hasty conclusion. The incidents recorded in this first volume are based on actual events and Horatio was an actual person; although I have to admit to clothing his character with some embellishments as to his origins and detailed behaviour.

That Horatio Evans was someone special is not in doubt and there are many men (mainly) like him. It is said that the male of the species is designed to pit himself against nature, to take risks, so as to advance the species and expand its skills. This may not have been precisely the motive driving him, but many of his actions and intentions could be explained by such a forgiving description. In which case, he emerges as something of a hero.

In other instances, where he would pit himself against quite ridiculous odds, aiming at unimaginably ambitious outcomes, he emerges as an idiot. I leave the reader to decide which fits him better overall. Whichever category into which he falls, the town in which he established his family was never the same after his arrival and stories of him continue to permeate the Welsh valley in which these scenes take place.

In case the reader wonders why I consider Abertump to be such a 'lovely town', the reason lies not in its physical characteristics, because like so many industrial valley towns it was, frankly, not attractive. There was nothing remotely bucolic about Abertump. To an outsider, someone who was accustomed to appreciating the soft rolling countryside of the Cotswolds, say, may think the town resembled a smouldering meteorite that had created a large crater, the deep valley, in which people scrambled about trying to make a living. It was still emitting smoke, from the mines and from the chimneys of the toilet bowl factory. They may believe its crater, formed by the steep sides of the valley, bear witness to the force of the impact, scarred as they are by black, pyramidal heaps of coal waste and the almost total absence of trees or, indeed, anything containing chlorophyll. Abertump looks as though it was built in a hurry, to house the termites labouring underground.

But for all that it was indeed a lovely place, for it, like so many Welsh mining towns, held a secret: most of its inhabitants belonged to an underground resistance movement, a movement dedicated to defeating the effects of hard labour, ill-health and dirt that the invading coal industry imposed upon them. The movement's victory was a subtle one: it took the form of a special humour and neighbourly goodwill, both of which were worn as a cloak to keep out the damp, the dirt and clogged lungs.

This first volume is but an introduction to this underground movement using examples from Horatio Evans's attempts to improve his lot by upgrading his home, a set of DIY disasters that if taken seriously would normally produce tears, but in Abertump many tears are dispelled by humour.

In later volumes we shall follow his increasingly quixotic ambitions and their accompanying disasters, from which he always seemed to extricate himself, albeit with considerable social upheaval and significant collateral damage. His disdain for all establishment figures, notably his teachers, the chapel minister, the police, the town council and Abertump's great land-owning family, the Fogles, provide Horatio with many opportunities for exercising his communist principles. He had a simple obsession: that he was placed on this earth to shake up Abertump and establish a new social and political order in Wales if not the world. The coal industry may well have had a negative physical impact on the once beautiful valley, but he was determined to light the blue touch paper of changes that would modify the town socially too.

***

The real Horatio provided an inexhaustible source of interest, amusement and sometimes dread for the greater family in which he and I were members. And we all loved him. I hope you enjoy this introduction to the man and the legend.

Ray Noyes, 2017

A HERO IS BORN

Horatio was born on a Tuesday, which is a happy coincidence, since Tuesdays were bin days in Llanelli: days that would be crucial to the lad much later in life. Little did his parents know the significance of the happy event that struck the Evans household on that day in 1939.

1939 signified the outbreak of hostilities, not only between Prime Minister Neville Chamberlain and Reich Chancellor Adolf Hitler but also between Lavender Evans, Horatio's mother, and Arthur his father; hostilities that were to have a profound effect on the life of their son Horatio Evans.

Arthur and Lavender were not well matched. He, a humble wheel-tapper in the local railway sidings came from humble Welsh stock and was proud of it. His bushy, Stalin moustache and semi-bald head reflected someone who was ordinary, someone content with his lot, not going anywhere soon.

True, tapping wheels was not going to get him very far, or stimulate his intellect much; but it was an important function and one he believed in. He had convinced himself that his work was a calling, not a job; otherwise he couldn't have stuck at it. He was sure that checking the soundness of a train's wheels was something that passengers using the Llanelli to Swansea line would be profoundly grateful for, if only they realised it was going on. The somewhat secretive function was a disappointment to him, not alleviated when he returned home to his wife Lavender in Tinplate Terrace, where she preferred not to acknowledge that she was married (she preferred the word 'shackled') to a husband whose zenith of his career involved bashing wheels with a hammer on a dirty railway.

Some passengers may occasionally have wondered what the clang of his hammer signified as he struck each wheel in turn at Llanelli Station or at the remote sidings, but he had long accepted that few did. He knew that his work was essential but unknown to the majority of passengers.

In spite of this, he managed to pull himself

out of his marital bed each morning at 6:30 and make his way to the depot to pick up his long-handled hammer with its small head (a tool which resembled his own physiognomy, for he too was long in the body and small of head) and seek wheels on the carriages of trains to receive his careful and expert percussive ministrations.

Such men made British Railways what it was, he told himself. There were no cracked wheels on the trains between Llanelli and Swansea just because of his expertise, surely this was worthwhile? This was his *raison d'être*: he, if no-one else, knew the importance of his work and he hung onto the thought like a bad swimmer to a life belt.

It had to be so, because those uncountable taps each day were his only defence against his darling wife. Without tapping wheels, his wife would be tapping him, taller and stronger as she was. In fact, Arthur only became fully Arthur when he was tapping wheels. Otherwise, he was just a humble serf, ruled over in their small two-up, two-down terraced house at number 34 Tinplate Terrace, by his darling wife, Lavender.

To Arthur, no two wheels were the same. Strange to say, that although healthy wheels were those that gave a pleasant, reassuring 'ring' when tapped, his inner rebel was always secretly and ashamedly delighted when he found one that responded with a dull clank. Like a thief, waiting for the opportunity to commit a crime, he would wait patiently with eager anticipation, listening to wheel after wheel, for that telling noise to sound out. Since neither he nor the value of his work was recognised, from time to time he could savour the secret power that he held in his hand, the power of finding a defective wheel. He felt like a miner finding a diamond.

These rare finds lifted his spirits as though he had committed a forbidden sin and it was something his wife needn't know about either. It was his secret and his alone, until he took his yellow chalk and made a cross on the wheel, showing the maintenance gang it had to be changed. Only then did he go public with his find.

So although to the casual observer and to his rather liverish foreman, he was the diligent, honest tapper of wheels, the guardian of safe travel on the railway, he had a demon on his shoulder; a demon intent upon welcoming into its kingdom a wheel gone wrong. In fact, he had occasionally found himself hesitating about using that lump of yellow chalk; what if he ignored that cracked wheel? Oversights could happen, after all.

At such times he savoured at full strength the power he held in his hammer hand. But chalk it he did, always. His working class sense of honesty and the professional integrity of his craft would not allow him to be slipshod. (But it was a good, fleeting feeling, that sense of power!)

His wife, Lavender, on the other hand, came from different stock and occupied a radically different world: her family, the Ffotheringay-Smythes were from Bristol, an altogether different milieu to Llanelli. They owned and ran a successful florist shop in the Clifton area of the city. Its name, 'Flowers for the Lady', was painted in gilt above a dark green shop front in a posh area, one that could afford flowers. That their daughter should carry the name of Lavender was, to them, quite natural.

(Her mother always told her that their surname, carrying as it did a double 'f', was a sign of their ancestral greatness: in truth, her great-great grandfather had a bad stutter.)

How Lavender and Arthur got together (she never admitted to anything so common as falling in love) was, she reckoned, a mistake, which, like most things in their married lives, she kept pointing out. They met in 1958, both aged 19, when they were visiting Bristol Zoo, she with her mother in a party from the Women's Institute, he with some mates from the Engineers' Arms from Llanelli.

She had become separated from the virginal ladies of the WI and was lost near the penguin enclosure. Arthur and his mates, however, were next door at the adjacent baboon enclosure, laughing at them doing rather disgusting things (the baboons, that is) when he noticed she was looking rather distraught, probably at what the baboons were doing, which was clearly visible from the clean, white and somewhat clinical penguin enclosure.

Wishing to save her blushes, he offered to find the WI group, to the amusement of the (amazingly) still-sober gentlemen from the Engineers' Arms, and led her to the information centre near the zoo entrance. The girl at the centre had already been alerted to Lavender's plight by the chairwoman of the WI party, a lady by the modest name of Boadicea, one that encapsulated accurately her character.

Arthur was smitten! The rescue of this pretty damsel from the penguin enclosure and the sexual exploits of the baboons had set his heart on fire. He asked her the universal question, 'Do you come here often?' and then committed what was probably the worst blunder in his entire life, that of convincing her he was a trainee design engineer who was taking a degree at Swansea University. She would love Swansea Bay, he insisted, and painted a picture of endless blue skies and clear blue water lapping at the shores of Swansea beach, omitting to mention the sewage outlets.

In her darkest moments, Lavender admits that she was somewhat taken in by this 'working class' boy and his amusing Welsh accent and cursed herself for it. But she was at a rebellious stage in her life and didn't see why a fling with such a lad shouldn't be fun. Thus she was tempted to catch a train to Swansea and meet him for a day on the beach. Now Swansea beach is very large and it hides a number of rocky nooks and crannies on its west side, in one of which their baby son was conceived.

She, of course, was not only shocked at being pregnant, but appalled that it should be by someone 'common'. Her 'bit of rough' had turned out to have a rather significant 'downside', his social *milieu*. Her parents were not only horrified, but eventually cast her aside to pursue a future with Arthur on whatever terms he could offer. Good florists from Bristol would never contemplate doing what she'd done; she was an outcast, a mutant florist.

Everything was going wrong for her: her entirely false professional design engineer, who on marriage gave her the all-too-short and (horrors!) *Welsh* name of Evans, was actually just a wheel-tapper. ('Why on earth did he have to be *Welsh*?' her parents wailed.) Shame was not the emotion Lavender felt: it was anger! He, Arthur Handel Elias Evans, was going to pay for this throughout eternity.

Her first step in her lifelong campaign of revenge was to restore to the family some dignity by giving the child a decent name. No Dai, no Dick no Dylan would do; it had to be something that stood out and showed off her middle-class, English ancestry. Horatio Evans was born.

Arthur and his family were not happy either. His father was a fervent nationalist and didn't see why they 'should be cowering before the bloody English again.'

Middle names were bandied about, the Ffotheringay-Smythes refusing to be involved at all, having told all their friends and relations that Lavender had suddenly emigrated to New Zealand with a brain surgeon she'd met at a church bring-and-buy sale.

Eventually, Arthur's father hit on a plan: if Arthur went along to the register office to register the birth alone, he could add whatever names he liked and Lavender could do nothing about it.

And so it was that Arthur returned from the Llanelli office with a certificate that attested that he was the father of Horatio ap Llewelyn Evans. 'Let 'em stick *that* in their bloody florist's window!' proclaimed Arthur's father.

In defence of Arthur's deceit, he did resist committing a further misdemeanour, that of altering the child's surname by adding an 'ap' to that too, as suggested by his father; but Arthur judged it to be an assertion of Welshness too far and may even have been illegal. Besides, Horatio ap Llewelyn ap Evans would be one 'ap' too far and would have made a real mouthful of his tiny son's name.

On Arthur's return from the register office, Lavender asked to see the certificate. Against all the odds, Arthur managed to convince her that he'd put it in the bank for safe-keeping. She couldn't prove anything, but her innate ability to read faces, especially guilty ones (a skill undoubtedly inherited from her shop-keeping parents), made her feel intuitively uneasy.

Two days later her suspicions were confirmed when Arthur's father, never known for being tactful, asked her what she thought of the baby's names. The subsequent domestic scene was not a pretty one, as he recited them, slowly, placing particular emphasis on the baby's middle name of ap Llewelyn as he leaned into her face.

No-one had told her that the added 'ap'

meant 'son of'. Few if any fathers of sons born since Prince Llewelyn's death in 1240 had had the effrontery to claim that their son was his true heir. This did not bother Arthur's dad, who if questioned about it would assert that it was 'about bloody time someone did then'.

Not only was Lavender understandably offended at being deceived, but she knew little of, and cared even less about, Welsh history, so that this middle name was simply ridiculous. Besides, she couldn't even spell it.

Tears were shed for weeks and Arthur worked an awful lot of overtime. Little did he realise the effect that the alignment of his baby's name with a Welsh prince would have. The fact was, the world was not ready for Horatio ap Llewelyn Evans and the great expectations Lavender had of him. If her husband was a failure, her son was going to be a success. This was to be her revenge.

Llanelli didn't know it yet, but it must prepare itself to welcome greatness, she said to herself.

HIS FORMATIVE YEARS

That Lavender had married beneath her was something to which she could never become accustomed. And she was determined to ensure that her discomfort registered in most of what she did. Any attempt on her part to integrate into what she felt was a backward, Neolithic, druidic society was at best half-hearted and at worst determined to fail.

For example, try as she may, she could not bring herself to understand the emotions that arose in Arthur's breast when discussing wheel tapping. As for inserting the merits of her husband's job into conversations with other women, into which she may have inadvertently been drawn, she could not contemplate it. Such 'common' women actually talked on doorsteps, a position no self-respecting housewife should occupy. 'Why don't they have afternoon tea indoors in the parlour?' she wondered. How she yearned for Bristol, although she was supposed to be in Christchurch, New Zealand, the lie her parents hadn't even told her about.

'Maybe none of these women has either a parlour or a tea set,' she wondered, ignoring that she was bereft of them too. Offering afternoon tea was certainly something that her neighbours would never understand, when they could just as easily (and cheaply) stand on their doorsteps in Tinplate Terrace and natter away, each of them nursing a chipped, 'liberated' British Railways mug.

So many were the offences offered to poor Lavender by this way of life that she was sometimes overwhelmed by them. She could see faults everywhere: faults in behaviour (what her mother would have called poor etiquette); faults in housekeeping (why were so many houses so dirty?); even faults in the shops which had, to her way of thinking, pathetically limited choices available and of such poor quality.

An example of this occurred about six months into her stay at Llanelli. She decided to make an attempt at being civilised and decided to cook Arthur a special meal. For this she needed spaghetti, natural, dried spaghetti, which she asked for at her usual grocer's. His reply floored her: 'Which one d'you want, bach, 'oops or alphabet?' She simply could not bring herself to buy a tin of either and walked home totally dejected. Her attempt at bringing Bristol's sophistication to Tinplate Terrace had failed.

Her neighbours, whom she had once hoped would be a source of friendship, never rose to her high standards and so never made it to her pantheon. They even wore aprons (not always clean and sometimes torn) *outside* in the street; or they put their hair in curlers and wrapped their heads in scarves rather than having their hair 'put up' at the hairdresser's.

And so, very quickly, it dawned on Lavender that such things as those to which she had been accustomed – good quality fresh fruit, a weekly visit to the hairdressers and to a department store – were not only unaffordable for her neighbours, they were unavailable.

Llanelli was a little slow in catching up with these things. The worst part of it was when she realised they were not only unaffordable for the people of Llanelli, but for her too. This was the cruellest blow of all: she was now an ordinary Llanelli wife, with an ordinary Llanelli husband's wage packet.

The whole tenure of Llanelli life was anathema to her. There was the language for one thing: not only did most neighbours, shopkeepers and the like speak this alien, out-dated ancient language, but their English was appalling. The use of strange terms such as 'over by there', 'where's it to?' or 'we do *do* something' was so irritating that she refused to get used to it. Her relationship with the people of Llanelli was not improved by her pointing out how badly they spoke and even correcting them. As a result, she could not mistake hearing herself described as 'stuck up' and frequently hearing the question: 'Who does she think she is, the little madam?'

But perhaps the most annoying thing of all for her, which sent her neighbours (especially the women) into fits of laughter, was when Arthur called her 'Lav'! We can easily imagine that by now her neighbours fully understood her distain for life in Tinplate Terrace, so that the tag of her nickname was just perfect for her. Even when Arthur tried to soften the term of affection by adding 'bach'; it didn't really work. Everyone knew that the Rubicon had been crossed, not least of all dear Lavender herself. She was marooned in Llanelli, with no way out. There was only one solution for her: to maintain a dignified distance between herself and the people of Tinplate

Terrace by staying indoors, closing her front door to the horrid world outside and trying her utmost to maintain her higher standards.

And so it happened that Lavender devoted all her attention to keeping Horatio indoors. She refused to use his middle names, finding difficulty in pronouncing its double 'l' in Llewelyn and dropped the 'ap' as an unnecessary and worthless appendage. She intended that he should be 'a somebody', someone of whom she could be proud. She would keep her eye on him and ensure he was protected against being infected by the social habits and poor language of her neighbours' children. Her intentions were good, but once again she was thwarted by the practicalities of such a scheme. Boys will be boys and unknown to her he mixed freely with others on the street. In fact, he was picking up not only their poor language but their social habits too, mainly the ability to fight. He had learned fast to defend himself, with his fists.

Horatio began school at the age of five with all his peers. Here we see for the first time the essential elements of his character emerging: he was belligerent. Even at such a tender age he often returned home with bruises and cuts after 'sorting out' another child or two. If Lavender had given up, he hadn't. His Llanelli life was only just beginning. He was becoming a Llanelli boy. His father, of course, was delighted. What a lad! Very proud he was, but not dear Lavender. Was further shame to be heaped upon her head by having a son who resolved disagreements with his fists?

The school, however, was not at all alarmed at Horatio's pugnacious character and felt that he was simply showing some 'character', some spirit. It was this very character that was to help him in later life as we shall see. He was destined to be a fighter of causes – most of them lost, but causes nevertheless. Some would later say he became a fighter *without* a cause, to the point where many people never understood why he was always in such a campaigning mood when everything around *them* seemed so peaceful and calm. It would seem that Horatio could make an issue out of anything, even those things that seemed to be running perfectly smoothly to the ordinary voter.

***

We now skip some years to when Horatio left school. His application to subjects academic had not been blindingly successful and he was advised, if not pushed (some say the headmaster begged), into leaving school and taking up a job. Once again, his mother resisted such a crass idea and felt that if only he could attend a better school, all would be well. But it was not to be.

There were no better schools on the doorstep and anyway the fees would be unaffordable.

Arthur took the hint when the headmaster called him in one day and offered to pay him (bribe him?) from his own pocket if Horatio were removed from beneath the hallowed roofs of the Llanelli Council Junior Mixed School, Slagheap Road, Llanelli. Of course Arthur did not tell his wife the full details of the interview with the headmaster, or of their son's resulting exit from the learned establishment; Arthur had accepted by then the need to dress up facts in sweeter, more positive terms for her absorption. (Lavender had no idea Horatio had become the best fist-fighter in the school.) He therefore told her that the headmaster believed that Horatio was far too advanced for his years and would be less bored by having a job.

If it hadn't been for her neighbours hinting at the real reason, she may have believed Arthur's story, but gradually the truth filtered through. She was furious with Arthur. As punishment, Arthur was not allowed in either the marital bed or even the house for several days for this lie, a period which he thoroughly enjoyed, living as he did throughout this enforced period of penury and banishment in the warm, friendly glow of the engine sheds amongst his mates. (How he later yearned for further enforced holidays of this sort, but few were to come his way.)

More disappointment for Lavender was to follow, because her son was to walk in his father's footsteps in pursuing a career in transport: in Horatio's case, it was road transport. He achieved this in a roundabout way via the army. Although he missed being called up for the war, he had to do a year's national service. He felt that his character which, it has to be admitted, had by now become primarily belligerent, was perfectly fitted for such a career. He'd also developed a rather loud voice and a tendency to emphasise his arguments by aid of a finger that prodded the air alarmingly and sometimes poked the listener in the chest. He could certainly get his point across, even if it was invalid.

The recruitment office in Llanelli high street was initially delighted that they had a customer, even one that had been called up, but as the initial interview proceeded doubts about him were expressed, behind closed doors. He told them he was glad to answer the call and join up because he had clear leadership potential, seeing himself quite soon as a regimental sergeant major, shouting across the parade ground to his battalion, a stickler for discipline and standing no nonsense from anyone. He told them confidently that given a little time he intended rising through the ranks to become a senior officer, perhaps gaining a VC in some war or other (perhaps one he'd started). But the army didn't want him to join as a driver of men, they insisted he be a driver of lorries.

It is difficult to say whether the army forged his character, or simply enhanced it; because his army service produced someone who was confident, strident, independent and, it has to be admitted, still belligerent. It was reckoned that his (self-acclaimed) knowledge of the law was one of his strong points and numerous were the occasions when he cited chapter and verse of army regulations at his corporal in order to get around doing something, either on his own behalf or that of others in his company. He had become the company lawyer.

This feature of his character, defending his own rights and the rights of others, tempted him to start up an army trade union, but his commanding officer didn't think much of the idea. (This was an idea Horatio was to take up later when he returned to civilian life. Trade Unionism felt like a good area in which he could specialise and use his undoubted talents of political persuasion and leadership.) It is not difficult to imagine that he was not the nearest and dearest friend of the company sergeant. The poor man gradually lost his nerve completely and was committed to an asylum suffering from nervous exhaustion and shell shock, although he hadn't been anywhere near shells; he'd just been near Horatio, but the effect on the poor man was the same.

Efforts to have Horatio removed early from the army failed, even when he appeared to have been caught red-handed doing dodgy deals; he was constantly thinking up schemes for outwitting the military authorities. As complaints about him escalated further and further up the chain of command, it became apparent that much time was being wasted by ever more senior people in simply getting Horatio to just drive his lorry and keep away from trouble.

His success at siphoning off literally thousands of gallons of diesel for the black market did not endear him to the authorities, although they were shocked at how easy he made it seem and as a result tightened up their security procedures for storing fuel.

When threatened with a full court martial, Horatio still didn't seem to be affected. He argued that if he was able to make the military authorities aware of how poor were their security procedures, perhaps he could be employed (at a higher rank) as a security consultant. He could have a bash at other schemes too and help them reveal weaknesses in their procedures. 'I'd be doing you buggers a favour,' he asserted to the tribunal chairman in court, 'just you think about it boyo, I've offered you a bloody good deal and it's staring you in the face, mun.'

But the chairman of the military tribunal was not amused and the poor man had certainly never been addressed as 'boyo' or 'mun', strange terms that he asked be translated for him. In fact, Horatio's suggestion and the way he expressed it may have contributed to the man's decision to hand over the case to someone else more in tune with such attitudes and language. The reader may recognise similarities between Horatio's behaviour and those of the character Just William in all this. They were quite alike, albeit of different social classes.

As often happens in cases where the rule book doesn't seem to be any help in controlling such people, promoting them can sometimes be a solution, especially if promoted to something banal, safe and of no consequence. There were therefore whispered suggestions (albeit behind closed doors accompanied by much smoke and uncounted glasses of whisky) that he be promoted.

At first the suggestion was not only laughed at but totally ignored. The suggestion was so incredible that it surely could not have been made seriously. The very idea of giving Private Horatio *more* power was so frightening to those valiant men in his chain of command that it was the final trigger for a lieutenant's mental breakdown. Getting the demented man out of the ammunition store where he had locked himself for two days, without destroying half of Swansea was, it was later admitted, touch and go.

But weird things can happen and they seemed to happen pretty often to Horatio. Within the year he was indeed promoted, to 'Lance Corporal Evans, Fuel Supplies', or as his peers called him 'Evans the Juice'. This unfortunate nickname, which referred to his conviction for stealing fuel, was one he was strangely proud of, although it was really meant as a dig by his mates at his conviction. We see in this incident a characteristic which was to surface frequently in later years: what others considered failure, he considered a success.

Unfortunately, nicknames cannot be used by authority figures such as a commanding officer. But the colonel was determined to get the army's own back on Horatio and bided his time, waiting until he could use his ultimate weapon: writing out Horatio's final discharge papers, including a personal reference.

The colonel wrote a verbose essay describing the extraordinary and unnerving talents, of Private Evans, H ap Ll, number 862457. His soldier's record book containing his colonel's parting 'love letter' as Horatio described it, ran to three additional pages plus an appendix, ending in sincere wishes that 'We hope he'll go far.' (The colonel's writing hand shook as he placed the full stop after the word 'far', because he desperately wanted to add the word 'away'.) Horatio, reading the colonel's notes, felt quite proud: 'Well, he might be a stuck-up English knob, but he's taken a lot of trouble with this and I'm bloody proud to have served under him.'

Our hero now saw a bright future ahead of him in civilian life; the army had certainly noticed him and he was determined to fulfil his full potential. Even if the rest of the world saw his actions as odd, even disturbing, he felt he was treading a new, enlightened path, one that would confront injustice and banality at every turn.

The army did have some positive effects on him. He left with a more upright, some might even say arrogant, appearance. He held his chin up and wore a trilby hat rather than a flat cap. The trilby was tilted at a rakish angle, something for which he would be known for the rest of his life. He even stuck a peacock feather in it for good measure. In fact, so devoted was he to wearing a hat, he was hardly ever seen without one; he always wore it in the house even at meals. If he was hatless, he was either ill or dead. He only removed his hat in the privacy of the marital bedroom.

He also took to shining his shoes, although this stopped pretty quickly after he took his first job, where he was required to wear industrial, steel-capped boots. 'If I polishes these boots I'll look like a bloody copper,' he reasoned. 'Besides which, it's middle class to have shiny shoes.' This form of thinking was one of the earliest signs of his burgeoning politicisation, beginning with him joining the Llanelli branch of the Communist Party.

To help him fit in with such an organisation, he grew a moustache, just like his father, but Horatio's was thinner and sharper than his father's. Even though he thought so himself, his thin moustache, and the cocked hat with its feather, defined him somehow. He felt he looked like someone who was going places, even if he didn't have a clue just yet where that might be.

TAKING THE WHEEL

Once discharged (some say ejected) from his short stay in the army, Horatio launched himself into society armed with a particular skill: driving lorries. He loved them. If there was one thing that fired up his enthusiasm and lit up his eyes, it was a lorry. In his quieter moments of self-analysis, he admitted that being up high, above the crowd as it were, was his destiny, his rightful place, physically and metaphorically.

And it didn't matter what type, shape or function of lorry he drove, everything from long-distance articulated juggernauts to ash carts. Luckily for him, he didn't mind the latter because that is where he found his true calling. For him, driving an ash cart (or refuse collection and recycling vehicle) was indeed a vocation: ridding society of its detritus was a social benefit he was proud to perform as a true communist. He wasn't only a collector of rubbish, he was also a saviour, of things unwanted and unloved, as we shall see.

But we're getting ahead of ourselves. He married, aged 27, a slender girl by the name of Gladys who came from Abertump in the Swansea Valley. She was taller than him and of the same age, but frail. She appeared to suffer a number of unidentifiable illnesses, all of which were mysterious and imminently life-threatening. Hardly any were known to science. For years her life expectancy had been a matter of months.

Visitors to her parents' house learned quickly not to enquire after her health. Asking 'How are you, dear?' was fatal, because they'd be told in horrifying detail. The symptoms then described would be distressing to the faint-hearted, requiring them to drink several cups of sweet tea (sometimes with brandy) to recover from the shock. Many a visitor left the cottage pale and shaky; symptoms like Gladys's were not only unusual but terrifyingly upsetting. 'She won't last long, poor love. She's a martyr, she is, a martyr,' was the usual thought.

Gladys was one of several brothers and sisters all of whom remained in the valley once they'd married and so Horatio found that by marrying her he'd become a member of quite a large family. This cheered him. He, an only child, had missed out on siblings, uncles and aunts. His mother, Lavender, refused to let her Bristol family meet him; his father, Arthur, was an only child too. So here, in the unsuspecting mining valley of Abertump, was a ready-made family for him and as it turned out, a ready-made audience for his schemes, social theories and radical politics.

Their marriage was not without problems: the wedding ceremony itself being the very first. Horatio, although a solid member of the working class, had strong beliefs to do with all things social and spiritual. In short, he was against them. He felt that the accepted precepts of society were there to be challenged and in this he found his calling, one of several in fact, which he embraced with vigour throughout his adult life.

This quixotic side to his character was to get him into trouble, but trouble out of which he always seemed to slip. Unlike Don Quixote, he wasn't a well-read, titled gentleman but this didn't stop the comparison being made by all who encountered him. One has to wonder what influence his name, Horatio, may have had on his willingness to confront dragons and evil-doers of all sorts, real or imagined, political or social.

Meanwhile, the wedding had to be agreed

and planned. One thing Horatio and Gladys could agree on was that it should take place in her own town of Abertump. Lavender, Horatio's mother, didn't actually *say* she didn't want it in Llanelli where the neighbours would meet Gladys and her large working class family, but the choice of somewhere other than Llanelli did give her some relief from her chronic social embarrassment. She dreaded having her neighbours witness her adopted family from Abertump consisting of ordinary working people rather than middle-class florists.

Gladys wanted a simple, chapel wedding with just her family around her. Horatio, however, always conscious of the need to promote the cause of the proletariat, wanted a civil ceremony, attended by the Brethren from the Communist Party and as many of the town's dignitaries that could be persuaded to come.

An additional and rather special cohort he insisted on having as witnesses was to be drawn from the 'Buffs', the Royal Antediluvian Order of Buffaloes, which he had also joined when living in Llanelli. (One may wonder how he could join two organisations whose principles were so mismatched; but as we shall see, such dissonances were not to cause him the least confusion or sense of divided loyalty.) At the time of the wedding, he was just a junior Buffalo, a Calf in fact, but he had great expectations of moving up soon to the First Degree of Wallaby and even becoming the Great Bison (eighth degree) one day. Imagining himself in his full regalia as the Great Bison, sitting in the Master's chair at banquets filled him with ambitious pleasure. But he harboured doubts as to whether Gladys would be up to being the Lady Great Bison, or was it the Great Lady Bison, he wasn't sure?

It has to be said, that his brother Communists were not too happy about his membership of the Buffs. The Buffaloes were middle class and bourgeois, so much so that two of the Brethren suggested pointedly that Horatio should choose one or the other organisation. But he was one of those exceptional leaders who can convince members of the proletariat one day and members of the middle classes the next that he's one of them, both at the same time.

We can see that there was a clash of desires over the wedding: Gladys wanted no fuss, a simple chapel ceremony with a few family and friends; Horatio was going for the Full Monty with representatives of two worldwide organisations being there: the Communist Party and the Buffaloes and Gladys should be honoured, as *he* was, that they'd agreed to come. But love conquers all and Gladys caved in, which was to be a regrettable habit she was to repeat rather too often in their marriage.

The Brethren turned up in some numbers many carrying red flags (all expecting a free lunch at The Mad Shepherd pub) and they filled most of the front seats, asserting their God-given right that the poor should inherit the Earth. The Buffaloes filled the back of the chapel resplendent in their regalia, as though to hide their quasi-Masonic relationships. So Gladys did manage to have her preferred venue at least.

Chapel venue or not, there were just a few details that Horatio failed to negotiate with Gladys, her family or the presiding preacher: he was not allowed to wear his Buffalo regalia or his Communist beret during the ceremony, nor was he allowed a phalanx of red Communist flags under which to walk when exiting the chapel. And the organist refused to play 'The Internationale'. Otherwise, Horatio was a happy man.

The sandwiches at The Mad Shepherd were not as soggy as had usually been experienced and some beef sandwiches contained meat. The beer was excellent and was amazingly close, for once, to its legal specific gravity. Geraint had clearly put on quite a show for Horatio.

'Put on a special, proper brew for you 'Or','

said Geraint the landlord, as though accepting that his brew wasn't always what it should have been. (It was just as well that Lavender did not hear her son Horatio's name being shortened to 'Or', or her despairingly negative view of all things Welsh would have been complete.)

The Communist Brethren were suitably impressed by the 'do' at The Mad Shepherd, especially since it was free, their numbers having strangely exceeded that counted in the chapel. All went well at the pub, until a fight broke out in the car park between a member of the Party and two stray Buffaloes who asserted loudly that capitalism was here to stay and that Communism was done for.

'Why don't you Commies just pack up and bugger off?' they suggested. 'Communism is dead and buried.' The Brethren were not amused.

'These bloody bourgeois Buffaloes are taking the piss out of the People's Revolution!' one of them cried, 'They ought to feel what it's like when the workers rise up. Let's show 'em, boys!'

It was a degrading quarrel in which Buffaloes should take part, one of them being of the Second Degree (Kangaroo) and the other being their Alderman of Benevolence (first class) which, next to the Great Bison is the highest rank. Nevertheless, having been attacked, they gave a good account of themselves. A third Buffalo would like to have become involved, but his office as the 'Certified Primo, Third Degree of the Great Marmot' prevented this. So he watched from behind a door of the outside toilets.

In the end, brute force from the Brethren (and the hampering effect of smart suits and the clanging regalia worn by the Buffaloes) began to turn the fight in the Brethren's favour. Some regalia was ripped from two Buffaloes and the medal of the Degree of the Kangaroo was tossed into a manure heap. But the Buffaloes' revenge was sweet as they captured not only the Communist red flag (resplendent with hammer and sickle) but also a Brother's communist-style beret (with red enamelled star).

The flag had been fixed to the car park gate post, arousing much curiosity from nearby residents, some of whom believed that the long-awaited Welsh uprising was underway. Dai Bungalow (so named because he had nothing upstairs) who helped in the post office, was certain of it. He began preparations for the uprising by turning the Queen's portrait round to face the wall, something he'd been dying to do for years, but resisted, in case it gave the game away that he had nationalist 'leanings' when working for Her Majesty's Civil Service.

'I've been licking that woman's bloody stamps for 37 years; surely it's time to have our own back?'

It was clear from the way that the Buffaloes and Brethren fought, that poor Horatio was in a cleft stick; he belonged to both sides; but here was where his leadership skills came in; he called down shame on both camps and urged them inside The Mad Shepherd to resume the celebrations. But his pleadings did not meet with a ceasefire, which was a bit of a shame. Hostilities were strangely self-perpetuating; but calm did resume after several Buffaloes (led by Brother Kangaroo) drove off at speed in their cars, pursued uselessly by a few of the Communist Brethren who only had bikes.

At around one am the following morning, the wedding breakfast came to a drunken end. In this state it was now impossible to recognise a Buffalo from a Brother. All had shed their jackets, ties, and anything else setting them aside from the common man and were snoring away either on the floor or slumped in chairs. In fact, several deep relationships had been unwittingly forged between a Buffalo and a Brother, all of which would be a source of shame in the light of day.

Gladys and the other ladies had realised much earlier that the reception was deteriorating rapidly and left. They nurtured cups of tea, complemented by Welsh Cakes in Gwen's Café on High Street.

***

The following day Horatio had time for contemplation, as the healing process from the night before slowly took place, aided by large doses of Alka Seltzer. He realised that although he had been close to his father, and like him recognised his place in society, he was different since he had a special gift. He knew he had inherited a latent leadership gene from his mother, Lavender and was determined to nurture it. Just as Lavender and her colonial English family felt that their lives were to be lived out answering a higher calling than that of the working class, namely, that they were capitalists and born to lead; so, somewhere hidden in Horatio's genome, was a sneaky little gene that expressed the same characteristic, leadership.

This presented a problem for him: how to use this gene in an otherwise modest working class environment? How to be a leader for the Buffs and another for the Brethren? But why, he realised, should he limit his ambitions to those organisations? The whole of Abertump society needed a shake-up and there was no reason why he shouldn't be the man to do it.

'Needs a bloody bomb under it, this place do,' was an observation he frequently made to whoever, willing or otherwise, would listen.

In spite of his marriage to an Abertump girl, he didn't like the place very much. It was too small for him, too small a stage on which to strut. Mining was the main occupation, except for jobs on the Abertump Council, the slaughterhouse, or the toilet bowl factory; and things ground rather slowly there. In fact nothing much happened at all. Time ground even more slowly than in Llanelli. An indication of Abertump's sleepy approach to life was a headline in the *Abertump Herald*: 'Police Constable Loses Whistle, Enquiry Set Up.' It needed shaking up.

Thus it was, that although Gladys, her parents and siblings were relatively content with their lot in Abertump and the nearby mining villages, Horatio judged them to be the downtrodden lackeys, slaves even, of rich, exploitative, capitalist employers, many of them colonial English, which was, in his eyes, the most profound condemnation of all. He went so far as to imply (if that isn't too mild a term for the language he actually employed) that they should be ashamed of themselves for accepting such an awful yoke. A capitalist society was, for him, something inherently evil that had to be confronted. He was the man destined to do it. Confronting the global evil of capitalism was to be his sacred calling. And it would start in Abertump, why not?

'Gotta start somewhere! Karl Marx did, in the British Library, mind you, we 'aven't got a library.'

Since his thinking was now reaching a higher, more strategic level (defeating global capitalism single-handed is pretty strategic), he developed certain mannerisms that set him apart from the common man (unfortunately). Many great leaders did this, he argued. They speak in a certain way, or dress differently. Quite often they have notable mannerisms. Churchill had his cigar and a two-fingered salute; why shouldn't Horatio wave two fingers at people, too?

One of his specific mannerisms was his long-existing habit of poking the air when excited, which came to the fore when pontificating on political issues. He decided to enhance this eccentricity so that it became his trademark. Seeing him on the high street even from a distance, it was obvious if he was trying to convince some poor voter of the need for change. The first finger of his right hand would be jabbing the air and the listener, whose posture was always that of leaning backwards, was clearly trying to get out of the way, blinking his eyes as he did so.

Indeed, some listeners would become quite alarmed, as Horatio ap Llewelyn Evans leaned in closer to the listener's face to make his point, his fine moustache twitching, spraying his unfortunate victim with just a little spittle.

Poor Gladys, meanwhile, who was a simple soul, was not ready for the burgeoning of his leadership talents nor for his eccentricities, natural or artificial. She was completely lost and often distressed at her husband's thundering political diatribes (which were particularly loud in the small, low-ceilinged cottage of theirs) and just wished for a quiet life with which to bring up her children and nurse her mysterious ailments.

She also wished to be able to get on quietly with consuming her Woodbines in peace, which was very difficult since Horatio declared he didn't like people who smoked, not because it was unhealthy or made the house smell, but he believed cigarettes were made by capitalists in order to drug the poor and keep them under control.

In a Communist Party meeting he once declared:

'The workers are in eternal servitude to bloody capitalist fags and are paying the price.'

To which one of the Brethren disrespectfully shouted, 'Yes, they're three-and-bloody-seven pence now; they used to be two bob for twenty.'

As time went on, Gladys gave birth to two beautiful girls, the apples of her eye and, to be fair, those of Horatio. He was a proud man, their births adding another layer of pride to his growing achievements in life. But they presented him with a dilemma: he wanted them to have a good education and all the signs were that they were worthy of one; but what if they married someone from the managerial class? What if they even became professional people and took on the mantle of employers themselves?

This needed watching! The Brethren of the Abertump Communist Party (South Wales Region, Swansea Valley Division) would also be watching. Heavy is the (domestic) burden of leadership! In a well-intended attempt to keep his girls on the straight and narrow, he nailed a framed motto above the mantelpiece in their bedroom that read, rather menacingly: 'He knows your every thought.' The warning spoke from an embroidered 'tester' of delicate coloured silks that some virginal young lady had painstakingly embroidered many years ago. It was very faded and badly stained due to the rain and the seagull droppings falling on it, as it looked heavenwards on the local tip. The outcome was that the faded admonition now read: 'He knows you ... though.'

The girls promised their dad they would always remember this, whatever it meant. Horatio was not a man to split hairs and accepted their promise.

COUNCILLOR HORATIO EVANS

Horatio's natural gifts as a leader were to emerge into the full light of day when he was elected to the town council. He had expected a chain of office, but was told he would have to wait until he became the mayor. One of the Communist Party Brethren pointed out that all were equal under Communism and he should shun anything that placed him above his brothers and sisters, such as wearing a chain of office.

Horatio asserted that he'd only wanted a chain of office on behalf of the Brethren, but it didn't sound very convincing. (It goes to show that whereas we are all equal, some are more equal than others.) Notwithstanding the disappointment over the absence of regalia, he was prepared to give of his valuable time and energy for the good of the lovely town of Abertump.

We all know that there are a few essential services that councils need to focus on: one is waste collection and the other is the position and number of public toilets. The Brethren were particularly keen to install some of the latter because, they said, it would directly assist the suffering of workers in society. Horatio's approach was similar, but different. He had been waging a personal urinary campaign against capitalism for years, by relieving himself against the door of the bank whenever he could, usually at night of course. This act of rebellion gave him a singular political as well as physiological pleasure. Urinating on an icon of capitalism was an especially delightful experience.

Because of this liquid campaign, and his long-time habit of picking up discarded items from back lanes and 'saving' them, he felt singularly qualified to offer advice in both specialist fields: the positioning of urinals and waste management. In the latter because he had recently joined the honoured ranks of refuse collectors and in the former because he experienced at first hand the discomfort provided by an evening at the Buffaloes, where beer is the main attraction, and trying to walk home on a full bladder.

Meanwhile, his love of lorries had finally paid off; there he was, seated literally in the driving seat of a new multipurpose ash cart. It gave him a certain amount of power; after all, it was he who determined the direction in which the thing would go: another dimension to his burgeoning leadership role in society. Actually, if there was one thing that would annoy him it would be for his vehicle to be described as an 'ash cart': it was a Refuse Collection and Disposal Vehicle (Volvo Mark IV). He was generally pleased with it, but was quick to point out to his supervisor that the new Mark V had a number of features on it that he preferred and that if a suitable occasion should present itself, he would appreciate having one. The response of his supervisor has not been recorded, but it seems it was pretty short.

The reader may pick up echoes here of his stay in the army, and, sad to say, his first supervisor was not long in being given long-term sick leave for his nerves. They say he never fully recovered, but is reasonably content living well away from the Abertump depot, somewhere in Northumberland, in a nursing home. It is said he is a broken man. Bin day at the home is on a

Friday and he is sedated most of the day.

More of the adventures of Horatio and his lorry later, but for now we should pay attention to Horatio's input to the location and the number of public loos, with particular attention being paid to the route from the Masonic Hall, used by the Buffaloes, to his small terraced cottage. It was entirely coincidental that two new urinals were installed between these two points during Horatio's term of office to the 'relief' of many Buffaloes. Some Buffalo colleagues were so grateful for the new facilities, they suggested the urinals be named the Horatio ap Llewelyn Evans Urinals.

But his sense of pride and perhaps even a certain civic shyness (that wasn't always apparent) decided him against his name being cast indelibly and eternally in iron alongside the word 'urinal' besides which there wasn't enough room for his name. 'The Evans Urinal' or 'This Urinal was Erected by Horatio ap Ll. Evans' didn't seem right, somehow. He'd rather be remembered for something less ordinary and smelly. Given time, he'd think of something suitable with which the town could thank him for his achievements. An opera house perhaps?

There were a few women councillors who raised a stink about the urinals, as if they didn't stink enough (the urinals, that is). They felt they had a good case for one of the two toilets being for women; but they were defeated by a mass show of hands (many of which had never been seen in the council chamber before, although they had been seen in the Communist Party Social Club) that outnumbered the women's votes of 12, to 49 from the men (this, in spite of the total number of councillors being only 37).

And so two new men's urinals were erected. One was about 200 yards from the Masonic Hall and the other about 200 yards from The Mad Shepherd, both of which were about 200 yards from where Horatio lived, at 74 Slaughterhouse Terrace. The geometric and surprisingly triangular coincidence that these urinary equidistant positions presented to an observant voter was amazing. As one keen-eyed resident pointed out, the distance between the Buffaloes' meeting place and 74 Slaughterhouse Terrace just happened to be exactly the same as the distance between Slaughterhouse Terrace and The Mad Shepherd. That the two new installations would be equidistant between Councillor Evans's two watering holes and his home was claimed to be purely coincidental, an assertion made by the Council's anonymous spokesman (actually Horatio ap Llewelyn Evans) when interviewed by a reporter from the *Abertump Herald*.

The minutes of the council meeting at which these urinary installations were passed, recorded that Councillor H. ap Ll. Evans spoke inspiringly and emotionally about the 'painful' need for these installations and called upon the council to 'pass' a motion, which it did. Judging by the number of voters in the council building in support of the motion, it just had to be passed in order to avoid a riot. The public balcony was packed to overflowing and the size of the crowd outside was intimidating. Most of them were waving red flags and chanting 'We'll Keep the Red Flag Flying'. Others, who didn't know the words, just sang 'We'll Keep a Welcome in the Hillsides' which strangely fitted the tune, more or less.

So the Brethren won the day, which shows the power of democracy. As for improvements to the waste collection services of the town, these were to take place gradually as Horatio gained in experience whilst piloting his Mark IV around the streets. But in as much as his initial interest lay in discovering improvements that could be made, he very soon realised that the current method was in fact flawless; that is to say, it allowed the maximum amount of refuse to be collected in the shortest time whilst allowing opportunities for the in-vehicle Mk IV crew to take initiatives of their own, such as personally 'recycling' some of it, an admirable achievement.

Horatio's understanding of the term 'recycling' was actually much more advanced than the classical one: he and the two other 'in-vehicle crew members' of the Horatio Express (as he named it) trained themselves to take note of items thrown out, usually in back lanes, and rather than see them buried in the local tip, they were 'rescued' and found new homes. This was true Communist recycling in action. Consequently, there were a number of rescued items to be found in the homes of the Mk IV in-vehicle crew, always, of course put to good use; to understand which, needs a visit to Horatio's home, to take but one example out of the three homes involved in the innovative recycling scheme in Abertump. We shall learn most by looking into Horatio's home and the improvements he was making within.

THE CONSERVATORY

74 Slaughterhouse Terrace was a modest, vernacular dwelling in a group of ten terraced houses. They had been built in the middle of the nineteenth century and consisted of just two rooms up and two rooms down. It can be imagined that in order to house (and sleep) the family of four, space was at a premium. So Horatio was always puzzling over ways of expanding the Kremlin, as it was generally known.

One way was to construct a lean-to or conservatory out the back, protruding into the garden. There was enough room between the back of the house and the 'privy' to construct such a thing and he was determined to set about it. It often happens that a man endowed with gifts of the intellect is not well endowed with practical skills. This is not a firm and fast rule, but in Horatio's case it was absolutely true. He may have had a leadership gene, but the rest of his genome was missing, the one for building things. This, of course, he couldn't possibly be expected to know, but Gladys had often told him he had something missing.

Unfortunately, leaders can often throw themselves enthusiastically into the most insane and impossible projects in their determination to achieve their 'vision'. Napoleon and Hitler spring to mind. Horatio's vision was just like that: enthusiasm he possessed, suitable skills he did not. Events often conspire to defeat such people.

The outcome of his project was therefore rather different to that which he had envisaged; more to the point, it was *dramatically* different to the vision (nay, the Heavenly scenarios!) described and promised to his dear wife and two young daughters. These disappointments affected Gladys's health; not only because of the chaotic disruption to the home, but that she consumed significantly more Woodbines on such occasions.

In the particular case to be described, the family was promised, and all imagined, having a beautiful glass conservatory under which they would leisurely take their breakfasts luxuriating in the new, bright space Horatio had created. The sun would shine on them through the brilliant glass ceiling and they would be blissfully content as they looked out onto the carrots and potatoes growing at the back of the house.

The result was just a little different to that.

Horatio had developed the design of a new conservatory in some detail, but refused steadfastly to contemplate someone else building it. Above all, he could not stomach the silly notion of actually *buying* any part of it, not even a single brick. All could be found lying around back lanes, on the council tip crying out to be 'recycled'. The new edifice would have a glass ceiling of course and windows all round, sitting astride a low brick wall, an admirable and traditional design. In this case, it would not only provide a place to sit, cook and eat, but one in which to have a bath. The multipurpose aspects of it were inspirational. All he needed were the parts and a little effort and he'd have just the thing to enhance the cottage in which he and the family lived.

'I'm not paying any bugger to build this; I'll do it for nowt,' was the approach he adopted with admirable optimism. 'Why put workers' money into the pockets of bloody capitalists when we can do it ourselves?' he reasoned.

It must be admitted, however, that neither his wife nor the two girls shared his optimism; they even tried to dissuade him from the project, based on previous schemes that had all started out like this, but had resulted in near disaster. What they realised with growing anxiety, verging on hysteria, was that never before had he attempted anything so large and so ambitious. When he erected a shelf that regularly fell off the wall, it was as nothing compared with a house extension. The scheme would need alterations to the very structure of the house, not to mention plumbing and electrics of a fairly sophisticated nature. Optimism in the family seemed to have taken flight and was 'rapidly disappearing over the horizon with its arse on fire', observed Neville, their next door neighbour. (Neville read books and although he rarely spoke, whenever he did, he usually came up with a phrase that succinctly described a situation like this.)

In the little cottage in Slaughterhouse Terrace the atmosphere was tense and gloomy; but leaders rise above such things and Horatio's spirit was on the rise.

'I'm always worried when Dad's in this optimistic mood', said the eldest daughter; 'I think I'll move out to somewhere safe. Why can't he just be lazy like other dads?'

The first thing Horatio had to do was to see how many bricks he might be able to find with which to construct low, stout walls for the base. From such a firm foundation he would add a timber frame and glaze it. All pretty simple, really. Oh, and he'd need a water supply of course, and the odd bit of electricity, oh, and drainage and perhaps even heating. The list was getting longer than he first thought, but undeterred he continued scouring the detritus and junk of the town to find what he'd need.

The problem with such a varied source of material is that each little piece could well be rather different to all the other little pieces, making for a rather higgledy-piggledy effect; and in the worst-case scenario, the pieces just won't fit together at all. This is particularly true of plumbing materials. Joining an old lump of Victorian lead pipe to a piece of relatively modern copper pipe is not easy, especially if many such 'bits' (often no more than six inches long, *each*) are all that can be found, requiring many of them to make up anything like a decent length through which water might be persuaded to flow. Making such a hybrid, multi-jointed pipe carry explosive gas under pressure was another obstacle that he hadn't overcome yet.

One thing he was determined to avoid was

buying anything new and of the right length; all would be found lying around in the back lanes of the town. It'd just need a little time to collect it, that's all. Bricks for the low walls weren't too much of a problem: it was the cement to stick them together that was a problem. That was until he found three bags of cement that had been thrown out of a building site. The bags seemed a little hard, but surely that's what cement is for, to go hard. So they were incorporated into his dream.

One fine day, he had amassed a sufficient number of bricks that had been painstakingly carried through the house (it had no rear access, everything having to be wheel-barrowed through the living room) and he was ready to start laying bricks.

The sand was easy, he got it from Swansea beach.

'A bit o' salt never 'urt no-one and the bloody stuff's free.'

It should be noted that an article in the *Swansea Post* that week expressed puzzlement that an Abertump Council Mk IV ash cart was spotted at low tide being loaded with sand by three employees. The Council (actually Horatio himself, as a councillor, writing on Council notepaper) responded by pointing out that the promotion of good relations amongst ash cart teams of the two towns was a good thing and was encouraged by the latest EU directive on recycling. Flying the Abertump flag on Swansea's beach was all part of that. No reason for the large hole left in the beach was advanced by the article.

Eager to start and even more eager to finish, he decided against digging up what he considered the rather attractive and solid York Stone paving at the back of the house and digging foundations; having jumped up and down on the flagstones a couple of times, he declared:

'Solid as a rock, better than any bloody foundations. They knew what they were doing when they laid these things.'

Foundations were declared unnecessary. This was yet another example of his deep insight into all things structural.

We needn't follow his construction technique brick by brick, suffice it to conclude that the edifice was 'interesting' to say the least. Not one to be constrained by straight lines or verticals, the walls were consequently an *approximation* to the base of a conservatory. Any changes to levels or to ensure straight lines would be made when he fixed the wooden structure on top of it, he reasoned.

'That's the mistake too many bricklayers

make,' he asserted, 'they're too keen on levels too early. The best place for getting it level is at the end, not at the beginning. That's what everyone sees after all, the finished job.'

Which seemed strangely logical to his mates and poor Gladys, but they couldn't figure out why.

Wood was easy to find, but straight, workable wood was not. The wood he'd found was not of the latter category; but ever inventive he used what he could get. This meant that different sections, lengths and strengths were blended together into an eccentric structure, which also incorporated windows that had appeared in back lanes and on tips. Being of different sizes, these windows required a creativity of which many carpenters could only dream. The net result was not so much a lean-to, as a 'lean-over'. Bulges here and there merely added to the work of art that spoke of creativity of the highest order. And it hadn't cost him a penny. Why use modern double-glazed units for the roof when old windows would do? After all, they were made to last:

'Not like the bloody nasty stuff today; they knew how to make windows when these were made.'

The fact that however well made they had been and that they had not been intended to be used as part of a conservatory roof, was of course a minor weakness in his argument. Sash windows, especially, disliked being installed almost horizontally.

It was not to be expected that such an eccentric structure was either strong or waterproof, but it had a certain attraction, especially to people who live in yurts, tents, tepees, grass huts or similar curvilinear structures. The absence of true verticals, straight lines or horizontals was actually praised by Horatio as an indication of its uniqueness.

'Ask any surveyor and he'll tell you how difficult it is to build something that isn't straight.'

He was right, of course.

This concept of curvilinear 'added value' incorporated into the design was something lost on Gladys and the girls; but was a source of boasting by Horatio, especially when the structure which, it has to be said was becoming notorious across the town, was inspected by his communist brethren and, more importantly, members of the Antediluvian Order of Buffaloes. The ceremonies of the latter, it is well known, emulate the building of holy temples in ancient Egypt, so that verticals, horizontals and building skills in general are of great interest to them.

As far as the Communist Brethren were concerned, the lean-over was a proletariat masterpiece: a fine example of the working class's struggle against capitalist property-owning bourgeois methods of construction. The downside of this strange structure was that the inside failed to present a straight surface of any kind against which to construct, say, a kitchen counter or a seat, or against which to place any item of furniture. But, undaunted, he merely took a hatchet to an offending bulge and got rid of it. It was so simple, really and rapid.

The ceiling too, possessed novel and downright fascinating points of interest. For example, it was not all of the same height. Indeed, one part of it, the central component, was several inches lower than all the rest. Horatio put this down initially to what he called lamentably poor workmanship (his actual words were slightly stronger than this) in a very old stained glass window that he had found. This amazing window had been 'rescued' from an empty chapel which was up for sale. The picture in the stained glass window was of 'Jesus Walking on the Waters', which seemed to Horatio to be a perfect metaphor for his own unique gifts to the world of architecture. Sometimes he was so confident he felt he could walk on water too.

Being very old, and meant only for mounting vertically, the stained glass window's sudden exposure to the horizontal meant that the slender lead strips holding the glass had sagged and even threatened to fall out. Horatio cured the problem simply and quickly by nailing a sheet of strong, clear plastic beneath it, thus preventing the glass from falling out or if it did, the plastic would catch it.

'There aren't many conservatories with a stained glass roof, so I'm buggered if I'm taking that one out!' was the reply of a confident and proud man. 'Look at the colours in it! Bloody marvellous!'

It was just ten days after the final old window and piece of rough timber had been nailed into place (rusty, used nails were a real hindrance, most of them having to be straightened out) that the first rain fell. The results were not reassuring. Several buckets were employed to catch the water that penetrated the structure but that could be sorted out. Some old cast iron guttering was placed at those points *inside* where there was most ingress, channelling the water *outside* through the open door. What he was going to do if the door had to be closed in winter, Gladys failed to understand.

She was very sensitive and had always been

afraid of being burgled. The thought of having to leave the lean-over door open all night in case of rain sat rather uncomfortably with her. Horatio's solution of sleeping with a baseball bat under his pillow in case of an intruder was not sufficiently reassuring. Again, he had demonstrated the amazing simplicity with which his creative mind was working. It was one of those rare conservatories that had its rainwater guttering on the *inside* rather than the outside. What an innovation!

'People don't think things through, see? With the gutters on the inside, I won't need to climb onto the roof of the thing to do repairs' – something that was in any case structurally impossible – 'and I can see where the water's coming in, too.'

Which was yet another logical assertion that was very difficult to deny.

The next stage of the project was to install the plumbing and especially a bath. Until that time, the whole family had to use a tin bath in front of the fire: not a satisfactory arrangement with two growing girls in the family. But Horatio had things in hand. He had been gradually stockpiling scrap lengths of copper pipe and the odd tap and was ready to embark upon Stage 2 the water system.

A bath had been found in the nearby river so that presented no problem at all. That its enamel had long given up being smooth was not an issue:

'I'll just paint the thing. I'll recycle some white paint from somewhere. Tons of it 'anging 'round.'

But having installed neither foundations nor drains, he realised the bath would not drain out unless he placed the end remote from the plughole higher than the drain end and the whole bath would need to be higher than the outside paving necessitating a further brick under all four feet. Once the water was outside, where it went after that, nature would take care of, he argued, not having realised that his garden sloped *towards* the house, not away from it.

Having two bricks under the feet at one end of the bath and single bricks under the other meant that entry and exit to and from the installation could be a little awkward; but that was a secondary problem that could be solved later. Gladys in particular raised objections to this.

'Well, stand on a bloody chair, woman!' was his characteristically reassuring reply.

To be fair to her, her legs hadn't been too good these days. She was increasingly complaining about having contracted the embarrassing complaint of Heavy Legs. Heavy

Legs was a relatively new illness to Abertump. She was convinced she had it, after reading last week's article in the *Abertump Herald* written by its health correspondent. The correspondent was not actually medically qualified, but he did his best. In fact the anonymous advisor on all things medical was Goronwy Davies the slaughterhouse foreman, a man singularly experienced in all things visceral, even if they were learned from dead sheep.

Unfortunately, the bath taps that Horatio had rescued from the tip were not both of the same type. In fact one was an outside or garden tap and the other was a stopcock; but that did not deter him from realising his objective. The outside tap he augmented with several additional fittings so that it would eventually connect to a suitable copper pipe that he was certain to 'liberate' from somewhere soon. He was a great believer in having faith, something would always turn up, even copper pipe. He did, however, admit to himself that the addition of so many extra brass fittings ('adaptions', he called them) had made the garden tap extremely heavy. In fact, he reckoned that the complex assembly would need supporting. But he didn't want to cross his bridges before his eggs had hatched and would sort that out later.

The stopcock was much more challenging: it

had clearly been installed for many decades in an old house and was almost impossible to turn. Whoever 'liberated' the stopcock had not bothered to free it from its lead piping but had just cut the pipes either side of it, which were still firmly soldered into the brass body of the seized-up device. He admitted secretly that this had him baffled at first. Either he had to remove both pieces of lead piping by heating the stopcock (but then he didn't know how he would connect the wished-for, hoped-for copper piping to it); or, and this was his preferred option, he would have to find a way of connecting the (wished-for, hoped-for) copper pipe to *one* side of the thing whilst beating out the lead on the other side into a shape that resembled a spout. Such a direct and simple solution was nothing short of plumbing genius (he claimed).

The latter solution he was quick to execute: a few blows with his faithful hammer from the coalhouse changed the shape of the lead immediately, in fact rather significantly so, so that the end of the lead pipe was now almost completely flattened and therefore partially blocked. It was a shape not exactly as he'd envisaged, but he argued that the water would find a way out somehow, probably in the form of a few jets, or with a bit of luck, a spray.

'All bathrooms 'ave showers now, this'll be ours.'

But he could not avoid having to face up to joining the remaining lead pipe on the other side of the stopcock to a length of copper pipe. He couldn't rely on the coal hammer to help him solve *that* problem. One day, he was rummaging around in the back of Mr Jones's ironmonger's shop ('Jones' Emporium Suppliers of All Things Sanitary to the Gentry'), when he spotted something entirely new, Super Glue. He had never seen this before and according to the write-up on the packet, it 'glues everything, from glass to ceramics, from copper to lead'. The latter description stood out like the light outside The Mad Shepherd on a dark night: it would do precisely what he wanted, join copper to lead!

He left Jones' Emporium with his new, super solution to an old problem.

'Modern science eh? Bloody marvellous!'

Then, as sometimes happens, Lady Luck smiled on him even more brightly. One of his Buffalo friends called at the house and gave him a length of brand new copper piping that was left over from some work he had been doing on his own house. He was elated, a condition much feared in the Evans household. That evening, he celebrated generously at The Mad Shepherd. His fellow celebrants, always keen to know the latest developments in the construction of his lean-over, were treated to a robust description of his latest round of inventiveness, which had been enhanced by the gift of four feet of precious copper pipe by one of his mates who was now drinking more than his fill of Felinfoel's best bitter (from Llanelli, of course). And, innovation of innovations, he'd discovered Super Glue!

Strange to say, Horatio was surprisingly challenged by the unexpected gift of copper pipe. One thing he could not abide was waste, he saw enough of it every day. This philosophy, admirable though it may have been, was to be severely tested by this length of new pipe. The pipe was a beautiful object of shiny, virginal copper; how was he to use it without cutting it and creating waste? The answer resulted in an installation that once seen was never forgotten, he refused to cut it at all and used all four feet of it so that it stuck out of the wall by its full length and reached way beyond the centre point of the (sloping) bath.

'I've never wasted such beautiful stuff before and I'm not starting now. Cutting this stuff is a crime. Some poor proletarian sod made this and I am not going to insult him by cutting it up.'

But he didn't mind cutting off some of the

short length of lead pipe from the stopcock and gluing into place a short, rather dirty, six-inch length of copper pipe. The gluing operation went so smoothly and so quickly it was a pleasure, although the first two fingers of his left hand took some prising apart. And so the stopcock was almost ready for installation.

He managed to fix it to the wall by cementing it in place. This simple solution also meant, he realised, that if the glued joint failed, it would be held together inside the wall. It did, however, mean that the tap was almost an integral part of the wall, making operating it rather difficult. More importantly, being in the wall, rather than over the bath, the spout was not now long enough to direct water into it. The addition of a chute of bent zinc beneath the tap solved this problem straight away, creating a hoped-for waterfall, a design that has only just been developed in the last decade, which shows conclusively how much in advance of his time he really was.

The hot water tap, with all its heavy brass 'adaptions,' was easily attached to the end of the four feet long length of new copper pipe, directing its water (when once it worked) well beyond the centre of the bath. Whilst this would certainly enable a user to add water to the bath, it made it extremely difficult to enter the bath afterwards. The bather would have to ease themselves under the long pipe with its tap and complex array of adaptions, and also try to avoid them whilst washing. At a guess, the tap and its adaptions would be situated roughly over the navel of most bathers. When one realises that it was impossible to support either the tap or its long pipe it meant that once the tap was turned on, the jet of water would lift the installation, spraying water in various directions as it bobbed up and down. On turning off the tap, it would also bob up and down for some time until coming to rest in a gentle arc determined by the mathematics of the laws of gravity and mechanical inertia.

Horatio decided to ignore these theoretical issues and focus on his primary objective: that of having water coming out of taps. He was not going to worry about the pathetic arguments advanced by the females in the family that it wouldn't be nice, or even possible, to use. But before the bath could be used, it needed hot as well as cold water. The solution to generating hot water was found at the back of the bus station, where some generous, altruistic person had dumped a cracked, cast iron wood-burning stove with one leg missing (the stove, not the person). Fitting such a stove with a tank of water that would be warmed by the stove's heat would provide the hot water supply required. Simple!

But where to put the stove? It may seem odd, but the centre of the garden was chosen as the 'obvious' place for it. Away from the delicate structure of the lean-over, its chimney would carry fumes away from the house. A brick or two under the missing leg would sort that out, and it would not be too far from the fuel supply which was to be coal. Wood, he argued, would not last long enough and there were 'tons of bloody coal under Abertump', although his scheme for mining it was not far advanced at this time.

'See? What people don't know is that coal is just very old wood, so a wood stove and a coal stove are the same. 'Course, the bloody capitalists don't tell us that so we buy both. Makes me mad, that!'

Thus it was that Horatio attached a steel tank (once a car's petrol tank rescued from the Abertump Garage) to the rear of the wood-burning (now coal-burning) stove and got himself a hot water system. But another problem had to be solved: how to get the water to circulate through the stove's water tank? Rigging an electric flex from the light in the living room (the lean-over had not been equipped with electricity at that time) to a recently 'liberated' central heating pump, suspiciously still in its box and discovered at the back of Jones' Emporium, solved the problem perfectly.

The stove's chimney was a bit of a challenge, but a length of bendy, corrugated aluminium air conditioning trunking sorted that out, supported by no fewer than five bean sticks.

'Can't be too careful with 'eat,' he said.

And so the bath was ready for testing. The fire was lit (with wood to begin with and then coal) and the circulating pump switched on. Once the neighbourhood cleared of smoke (the fire station was in the next street and much anxiety was aroused within, but no-one had called for their help), much gurgling and banging could be heard from the apparatus; but gradually, over the space of an hour or two, the car's petrol tank full of water became warm.

The pendulous tap over the bath, on its long length of new, bendy copper pipe began behaving rather strangely. As the apparatus became warmer, the expected gurgling noises as the water tank became hot, became louder and more alarming. The unsupported and very heavy tap was seen to be moving up and down to the rhythm of the gurgling and rumblings and describing a quite alarming vertical arc on its four-foot length of pipe, until it threatened to hit the base of the bath.

Ever resourceful when called upon, Horatio tied up the tap and the long pipe to the ceiling of old windows with string.

'See? 'Avin' wood windows on the roof means I can stick a bloody nail into 'em. Can't do that with fancy aluminium windows!'

The tap, its adaptions and pipe suddenly appeared more sound that way, less temporary, perhaps. String can do that. The gurgling and rumblings having reached a pitch, Horatio decided it was time to fill the bath with hot, fresh, cleansing water. He'd worked hard and a bath was just what was called for.

The taps were turned on....

What emerged from the hot one surprised everyone: it was a very dark brown, the colour of well-stewed tea, carrying with it deposits of dirt and rust that spread out on the bottom of the bath and splashed over the 'bathroom', as the tap, its adaptions and its long pipe broke loose from the string and oscillated up and down threateningly. The old stopcock which was supplying cold water down its chute, suddenly decided it didn't want to do that anymore and shot out from the wall, separating from its glued joint and landing at the other end of the bath. No-one was concerned that it may have marked the bath's enamel because there wasn't any. But the jet of high pressure cold water from the fractured pipe within the wall was now hitting the far end of the bath and was splashing everywhere.

It was a source of some puzzlement that the floor of the lean-over was also getting very wet, but not from the splashes from the ruptured cold water pipe; the water was coming from outside. The drain on the sloping bath had worked quite well but the garden was refusing to soak up the water and was insisting it flow towards the house.

Meanwhile, out in the centre of the garden where the stove and makeshift boiler were shaking and smoking, surprising things were also happening. Firstly, the bean sticks were alight. They had given up on the improvised, hot chimney, which was melting and had drooped like a wilted flower, spewing obnoxious smoke onto the garden at low level like a vacuum cleaner put into reverse. What he thought was aluminium was in fact plastic and it was on fire.

Secondly, as the hot water left the system through the oscillating tap, cold water entered the tank back at the boiler to replace it. It seems the plumbing was not prepared for this, and it began to creak and groan as it received the sudden shock of cold water. The noise grew louder and suddenly turned into a booming sound as the cold water entering the tank behind the stove stirred up some residual petrol that expanded explosively fast and made its way down the pipe and out through the hot water tap at high pressure.

Even Horatio was not prepared for what happened next: the petrol fumes caught fire from Gladys' Woodbine and the family were treated to the very unusual sight of both water and flames issuing from a tap, which snaked about like a wild animal. It was as though the water itself was on fire, the tap's dragon-like oscillations distributing fire and water everywhere, including onto Gladys whose apron was badly singed. Her Woodbine had been extinguished and re-lit twice in the space of a few seconds.

The family stood in stunned silence. Gladys had one of her 'turns' and retreated to the relative safety of the living room where a large supply of tablets and potions were available to treat her conditions. The thought of once again nipping next door for a whiff of Neville's oxygen bottle resurfaced. Fresh Woodbines were drawn by her trembling hands out of her apron pocket but failed to calm her nerves. Slouched in one corner of the settee, she was heard to emit a mixture of high-pitched, hysterical whimpers, rather like those of a distressed puppy, accompanied simultaneously by deep bronchial coughs like those of a miner: simultaneous feats of which many a ventriloquist would be proud.

The girls meanwhile, moved outside into the back garden to avoid the flaming water tap, but immediately realised they were then close to the thundering, overheating stove and its improvised petrol tank of a boiler. They ran through the house and sought refuge with friends nearby, not sure whether the situation was funny or grave. If the truth were told, they were not only shocked but angry, that their dream of a bathroom in a pleasant glass conservatory had ended like this.

But Horatio was up to the challenge. Initially he tried to turn off the flaming tap, but having burned his fingers he grabbed a tea-towel and tried again. Unfortunately, the heat had hardened the washer in the tap and it refused to close. There was nothing for it but to halt the flow of the mixture of water and gaseous petrol at the boiler. This too was fraught with difficulties because, wishing to economise on parts, he hadn't equipped it with a stopcock.

Bravery is one feature of leaders and Horatio possessed it in spades; or perhaps he was simply unaware of the dangers. Either way, he strode into the garden and with his trusty coalhouse hammer struck a blow on the outlet pipe which, being constructed Lego-like of many short, miscellaneous lengths of pipe, roughly soldered together, parted immediately. Jumping back from the flames and hot water, he fell backwards into a row of runner beans, ending in the middle of the structure, with plants and beans draped over his face. He had a surprised look; his eyebrows had reached the highest point on his face, making his eyes bulge like bloodshot beacons.

'Sod it! It wasn't meant to be like this,' he thought secretly to himself, but as he emerged from the runner beans and re-entered the house, his confident smile reasserted itself.

'Just a temp'ry setback, bach,' he told the gasping Gladys, 'just temp'ry.'

She wasn't sure whether to be consoled by this or terrified, because it could mean that he hadn't given up, and his struggle against reality could begin all over again another day. The family resumed bathing in the tin bath next day and washing in the kitchen sink, once they'd cleared away the debris of plumbing, bricklaying and a thick layer of dust.

As an extra safety measure the girls propped up the lean-over roof with three lengths of wood because the heavy if elegant Edwardian sash windows and the chapel's stained glass window had begun their combined slow descent. Their weight was clearly in excess of that which Horatio had painstakingly and carefully calculated for the fragile roof structure, made mostly out of orange and tomato boxes.

The chapel's 'Jesus Walking on the Waters' was certainly not as miraculously watertight as he'd thought. As a result, rain entered freely and the water level on the floor rose alarmingly when it rained, in spite of the innovative inner guttering. But it was a problem which he solved easily by stopping up any yawning gaps in the windows with expanding foam, another triumph of science, also discovered in Jones' Emporium.

Horatio was a master of improvisation; the problem was that his solutions rarely lasted longer than a day or so. Eventually, some two weeks later, Horatio considered the installation complete and fully commissioned. The installation of electricity is a story all its own, but suffice it to say that although his knowledge of the science was rudimentary, once finished, an electric bulb did glow dimly in the lean-over; although he felt he should issue a safety warning, that no-one should try and switch it on or off if they had wet hands or feet. He preferred, he said, that the old, Victorian china and brass switch he'd found ('Beautifully made them was, best you could get when they came out') was best operated by means of either rubber gloves or a wooden pole, both needing to be dry.

Unfortunately, the family refused to use the bath after all because he would not dismantle the pendant tap on its long length of piping, which meant that entry to the high and sloping bath was almost impossible unless the user were able to bend double and twist around at the same time under the four-foot pipe and its heavy brass tap and adaptions. The problem of drainage was still unsolved. Why the garden refused to soak up the bath water he found rather annoying.

'The bloody stuff sucks up rain alright, why not bath water?' he asked one of the Brethren, who hadn't a clue, he said. 'Perhaps that's why they 'ave drains?' the Brother queried.

His decision to preserve the gift of a new pipe intact showed that his appreciation of beautiful plumbing materials was highly developed and his sympathy with the downtrodden member of the proletariat who made it was solid.

'Some poor sod made that bloody thing, workin' under the cruel lash of a bloodthirsty capitalist. I'm *not* spoiling 'is workmanship now.'

The girls meanwhile agreed unanimously that the new lean-over was not a success, sagging as it was in the centre and of a rather rhombic shape overall, with yawning holes penetrating its walls. It seemed very different to the conservatory of their dreams and still left much to be desired in terms of water management. They realised they would have to wait a long time until they could luxuriate in a bath whilst looking at the stars through a clear glass roof even with 'Jesus Walking on the Waters' to reassure them.

To be fair to him, Horatio accepted that further detailed planning (and scavenging for parts) would be required if the project was to be a total success; notably, he must find a hot water boiler that had not seen petrol in its entire life. And perhaps find a more elegant solution to adjusting the slope of the bath than using bricks. A drain would be handy, too.

The talk amongst the Communist Brethren and his fellow Buffaloes was that he had managed to construct something which Abertump had never seen before, but which at any moment could either collapse or explode. But such was Horatio's force of character that no-one dared express any doubts about the integrity of the installation, at least to his face. Behind his back, expressions of amusement were rife. To make things worse, Gladys and the three girls had been offered the liberal use of next doors' bathrooms by both neighbours, out of sheer pity. The shame of seeing them leaving the new installation unused hurt Horatio deeply. He was at a loss to understand why his amazing DIY skills had failed to charm his family.

To him, this edifice, costing nothing and arising out of the ground uniquely as a result of his inventiveness and keen observation for discarded items (finding 'Jesus Walking on the Waters' was a master stroke) would have defeated a lesser man.

THE WARDROBE

It is said that pride comes before a fall, but in Horatio's case his emotional setting seemed to been stuck on 'pride'. No amount of criticism of his DIY efforts dented his feelings; in fact they seemed to have amplified them. His daily round of Abertump's back lanes in the company of his two in-flight crew members confirmed this. His lectures on the benefits of Communism and the awful state of Abertump had been replaced by ones on the benefits of DIY 'communist style'. As is the case with the finest leaders of men, he ignored criticism of his aims and ambitions and converted them to proof that he was on the right track and that everyone else was just plain stupid and didn't understand.

His confident view of the changes that

Abertump required were not restricted to the sensitive ears of his two-man crew; he took his strengthened convictions to the pub too, to The Mad Shepherd. There, amongst a captive audience ('captive' because drinking Geraint's odd beer was not something that could be attempted quickly) he sounded forth on the evils of capitalism and the corruption of the council, of which he, of course, was a member. This strange disassociation from the very cohort he was criticising was yet another demonstration of how leaders can put themselves at arm's length to a problem with which they are personally associated, rather like a surgeon being able to cut into the belly of his mother-in-law without flinching.

At home, he insisted on demonstrating the benefits of the new lean-over and its peculiar bathroom. He always took his baths there, filling it by hand as he had done when using the tin bath in front of the fire. Hidden from the family's delicate eyes were the contortions he had to use to enter it, but twist and turn he did, so that he managed to lie beneath the four feet of relatively new copper pipe with its several attachments and, of course, the garden tap.

As if to further endorse the worthiness of the thing, he usually sang, choosing rousing communist anthems rather than Welsh hymns. Neville next door, who suffered from a miner's chest and kept himself alive on oxygen, was not appreciative of these renditions; his main hobby was reading, and Horatio's voice was not conducive to creating a suitable atmosphere for the task. In fact, when Gladys occasionally popped next door for a whiff of his oxygen to help her own chest, he made it clear that singing of that nature ought to be restricted to the pub, to the hills or at the Abertump Communist Party meetings (South Wales Region, Swansea District).

But however Gladys communicated Neville's wishes, her efforts to silence Horatio failed abysmally. He was like a cockerel; he was king of the roost and was singing about it.

Taking a bath often gives birth to ideas and on one such occasion Horatio had another. 74 Slaughterhouse Terrace was not a large property; in fact it was a very small one. It had only two bedrooms and neither had fitted cupboards of any kind, so that free-standing furniture was needed to store clothes. Two growing girls sharing the same bedroom meant they had an equally growing collection of clothes; but a wardrobe there was none.

Until, that is, Horatio spotted one.

It was standing forlornly in the rain at the

back of The Mad Shepherd. The ash cart halted with a sudden jerk as Horatio's eyes lit up with the discovery that here was a prize worth having: a wardrobe for his girls. This admirable, if not touching sentiment, he nurtured all day, tainted however by the fear that 'some other bugger' might steal it. But he had a plan: one of the lads would have to hang about and guard it, until they had finished their round and the lorry had dumped its load on the council tip. Then, with the lorry empty, the desirable bedroom article could be transported to 74 Slaughterhouse Terrace. Simple!

The smallest of the three-man team on the Mk IV ash cart was Terry, a wiry little chap aged about 23. He was not one of Abertump's brightest voters, but he was good at taking orders, even if, as frequently occurred, he didn't understand them. His IQ was around 6, which would put his intellectual capacity somewhere between a pot of yoghurt and seaweed. He was faintly aware of his intellectual weakness, but it was more than offset by being a close associate, nay a devoted follower, of his hero Horatio Evans. It should not be thought that Terry worshipped him, but it was as close to hero worship as was possible to get in a town like Abertump, a town that had never seen one before.

And so it was that as the ash cart left the lane behind the pub, Terry (or 'Flash' to use his ironic nickname) was left alone with the wardrobe. It was quiet there, as the rain fell steadily. It took him quite a while to realise he was not enjoying himself. Standing there alone in the rain, unable to even light a fag, he had a flash of inspiration and decided he could do his sentry duty just as well inside the wardrobe as outside it.

'Why get wet, after all?' he suddenly realised.

This is how Terry (the son of a funeral director's assistant in the embalming department, and an immigrant from distant England) responded to most things in life: it took quite a while for things to sink in. Sad to say he didn't realise why his nickname was Flash: he thought his colleagues were comparing him to the then popular Flash Gordon, the cinematic hero, or perhaps were subtly implying that he was actually mentally quick. The use of double irony and the power of the *double entendre* were as yet unknowns to Terry. Of the two possibilities, he preferred to believe he was mentally 'quick', the definition of which, was uniquely his own. Sometimes it is cruel to disabuse people of their own convictions, false though they may be and Terry had been left alone in his contented belief about his mental agility, confirmed by deciding to enter the wardrobe.

The key to the wardrobe was missing, but the doors opened easily and in he slipped. Sliding to the bottom of one side of the piece of furniture, with his knees bent double, he was quite comfortable, although smoking his Woodbines in such a tight, enclosed space was using up so much oxygen that within the hour he was asleep. Luckily for him, no-one else seemed to want the wardrobe so he wasn't disturbed. A further stroke of luck was that the ash cart finished its round, in spite of being one man down, in record-breaking time. The effect on the streets of Abertump could be seen by a keen-eyed voter to have resulted in numerous dustbins remaining un-emptied. The Mark IV was capable of a fair turn of speed when pushed, a characteristic that was employed to the full in completing the round in record time.

(It was estimated by a retired traffic policeman that the Horatio Express had driven through the narrow lanes of the town at speeds in excess of 50 mph in places.)

The shift over, the Mark IV returned to the back of the pub. The wardrobe stood exactly where they had left it, albeit now rhombic in shape, being tilted to one side under Terry's weight, and emitting smoke from his fags. On opening the doors they found him puffing away on his last one and looking decidedly green. Smoke poisoning, it is said, is not a pleasant way to go. But Woodbine poisoning was an entirely new phenomenon and Terry was definitely showing its symptoms: the principle of which, besides a deep-seated cough, was a stupid grin on his face and an inability to realise where he was (although they weren't sure if that was actually a symptom or exaggerated normality). When told he was in a wardrobe he simply laughed, which must have been a secondary symptom of Woodbine poisoning. One must sympathise with him: after all, who of us when woken up and told we were in a wardrobe would at first believe the information?

He had to be brought round and there was nothing for it but to appeal to the good offices of Geraint the pub landlord in serving Terry (and why not the others?) a pint or two of his diluted brew. For good measure, Horatio decided that some of it should be poured over Terry's head but it only served to make him more disoriented. Eventually, the beer seemed to do the trick and all three men were ready for the final stage of the project, to transport the wardrobe to Slaughterhouse Terrace, at number 74. It was done remarkably quickly, although numerous scratches in the item's delicate French-polished body had appeared.

'You won't notice those after a while,' boasted Horatio, 'after all, it's about an 'undred bloody years old, what can you expect from antiques? It's called patina, lads, in the trade, that's what it is, patina,' he announced confidently and confidentially as though imparting a Masonic secret of the antiques trade.

Thus it was that poor Gladys, although having a bad day from her multiple ailments, almost dropped to the ground when the three lads appeared at the front door with their new-found gift. Collapsing onto the settee, she prayed aloud in Welsh to the good Lord to help her, as another Woodbine was shakily lit up and she began whimpering quietly. Horatio's surprises (she called them shocks) had happened so often that she knew with a certainty verging on perfect clairvoyance that it would end badly. She was even thinking of popping next door to have another whiff of Neville's oxygen bottle to 'help her chest'. Her asthma pump and two Valium did help a little.

'I needs morphine, I do, not bloody Valium. The pain, the pain... oh, God 'elp me; what's 'e brought in yer now?' was the sad restrain from the suffering Gladys, seeing her tiny home once again threatened by its lord and master's initiatives. It was actually a pity she didn't pop next door. The next hour or two were to be 'interesting' to say the least. Perhaps we ought to say dramatic.

Miners' cottages from the nineteenth century were not built for tall people, nor did they have much of a hallway. Basically, the front door opened into the living room, except for a space just big enough to open the door and perhaps accommodate someone squeezing their way out. The wardrobe, however, had been built for a grander homestead with taller ceilings and it was not going out, it was coming in. It must be said, in his defence, that Horatio managed what Terry reckoned was impossible: the wardrobe was tilted and tipped, twisted and turned and eventually there it stood, in the living room, more or less upright.

It was not, however, in one piece. Regrettably, it had been essential that the ornate (they thought ugly) carved headpiece atop the wardrobe be removed. None of them liked it and they were men of some discernment in these things having seen wardrobes before. The rusty coalhouse hammer removed it rapidly with only minimal tearing of the veneer on the front. They all agreed it looked an imposing piece. So imposing in fact that no-one moved, they couldn't, due to its size. Iolo reckoned its volume to be roughly a third of that of the entire room. Even without its Victorian headpiece, it almost touched the ceiling boards between the exposed beams of the cottage. So in order to move it at all, it had to be repeatedly tilted and shoved beneath one beam after another and only allowed to assume an upright position once it was standing between any two of the beams.

These manoeuvres demanded not only strength and teamwork but space. Space, however, was not a plentiful commodity at number 74. The settee on which Gladys had collapsed was taking up quite a bit of the precious stuff and was therefore unceremoniously lifted into the air and moved into the back garden with Gladys still on it. Her otherwise quiet whimpering moved up an octave and increased in volume by multiple decibels until they became screams. The two girls ran to pacify her, both of them accompanying her in Welsh prayers, knowing that they usually helped her calm down. Seeing her slippers becoming dirty from dangling in the carrots they lifted her legs onto the settee out of the way.

Meanwhile indoors, the desirable antique with its valuable patina (or deep gouges) was standing at the foot of the stairs, its dark menacing presence creating an atmosphere of doom in the room, as though a couple of very large, threatening policemen had walked in and wouldn't be moved. It was indeed intimidating. Its huge bulk shut out the light, the room made even more sombre by its deep mahogany veneer, what was left of it. It seemed as though Horatio was to be defeated. The stairs in such cottages are not straight; to save space they are steep, narrow and have a very sharp bend. Iolo, the biggest, slowest and most sensitive of the three men, began to edge towards the door, he was upset. He could see Gladys through the open back door in a state of total collapse (he was a sensitive soul and played the harmonica) and was worried she may fade away completely and with him as a witness. Terry too was uneasy, but was (typically) mystified as to why. To their relief, Horatio suddenly dismissed them both!

'Right lads, thanks for yer 'elp today, I'll sort out the rest. You can bugger off if you like.'

With no idea how he was to lift the thing up the steep stairs, both associates were more than glad to go home. The two of them escaped what they imagined would be a titanic struggle that might be awful to watch. They left as the wardrobe faced Horatio at his most determined.

Gladys, meanwhile, who was still outside in the carrots, had managed to stand, breathing in deeply to 'help her chest' and asked one of the girls to go to the shop to replenish her stock of Woodbines. 'Get forty, love, I needs 'em.' It seemed her prayers and appeals to Heaven may have begun to work. She felt a little better for being away from Horatio and out in the fresh air, although her once pink slippers with fluffy pom-poms on the toes were looking pretty sad. She and the girls, all three sitting on the settee, eventually realised that things were eerily quiet in the house, which was not only odd, but worrying. They poked their heads around the doorway and were puzzled at what they saw: Horatio was doing nothing.

He walked (squeezed) around the wardrobe, as best he could, sizing up the problem, literally. Gladys had to admit that although Horatio's constant 'innovations' as he called them, drove her to distraction, seeing him doing nothing like this was completely unnerving her. It was like waiting for a clap of thunder that never comes.

'For God's sake, don't just stand there, do something, you're making me scared,' was the only thing she could say, followed by several bronchial convulsions.

'Listen now, luv, it's no good rushin' into things and making mistakes. Too many people does that,' he replied. It was a statement that should have been cast in bronze, polished and erected over the mantelpiece of number 74.

'Good God he's bloody mad!' were the last words heard from Gladys as she grabbed the door frame and slipped onto a kitchen chair beneath the sagging roof of the lean-over, raising her eyes to Jesus Walking on the Waters.

The power of silence is an amazing thing, Horatio noted. Not believing in the arithmetic limitations inevitably imposed by actually measuring the size of the wardrobe, he called into play his amazing gift of estimating accurately three-dimensional space. (Dustmen are good at this.) And he came quickly to the conclusion that 'it wasn't going to go.' He didn't, however, vocalise this conclusion, even though the two girls, Gladys and the two other members of the Mk IV in-cart crew had already made the same observation much earlier. Leaders are often assailed by the doubts of their followers and have to learn not to listen to them. What Gladys and the girls were therefore witnessing was a leader in deep thought, weighing up the pros and cons, not being rushed into precipitous action. Either that or he was stumped.

Finally, he left the room and with slow, measured, assured steps made his way down the garden to his shed. This amazing construction had remained more or less upright for years, even though it had a distinct list to starboard. For that reason it was known as the Leaning Shed of Pisa. One of the effects of its inherent angle of inclination, was the difficulty of opening the door, which would strike the ground. The rest of the family had no desire whatsoever to enter it anyway (considering it too dangerous) so there was no risk of anyone taking anything of value, the most valuable item in it was a shovel standing in the far corner that he had 'liberated' from British Rail.

He disappeared into the depths of the peculiar edifice and emerged with a large rusty saw, at the sight of which Gladys had another 'turn'. She decided the only place she was safe was in the outside loo, which was another interesting building, but one that had stood for many years, being built by Victorian bricklayers. It was a place in which the occupant felt fairly safe. To be quite sure of her safety she bolted the door and was now well supplied with Woodbines.

Although Horatio didn't like smoking, the sight of Gladys' smoke leaking lazily out through the several vee-shaped cuts in the top of the door was somewhat reassuring, even poetic, he thought. It reminded him of a painting he'd once seen of a lonely mountain farmstead with smoke rising lazily from its chimney as the sun set. He'd always felt that the smoke in the painting implied that a contented state of family bliss reigned within. In the same way, he liked to see Gladys's smoke rising lazily from the brick privy, his interpretation being that Gladys was reasonably content and her bowels were working.

Horatio took the saw inside and looked once more at the dark, menacing presence of the wardrobe, like a judo contestant sizing up his opponent. He had a plan. If its height was a problem, he'd reduce it. He noticed it had four legs and these had to go. A few energetic cuts with the saw solved the problem, although not very neatly or evenly. The result was a leaning wardrobe: one that leant forwards as though admonishing the observer.

'These things'll burn well,' he thought, turning the legs over in his hands. 'Not needed these days. Don't need legs no more.' He threw them onto the hearth of the fire.

But the sheer bulk of the piece was still problematical. The stairs were clearly far too narrow, too steep and had a right-angle bend in them to accept such a thing.

'Removin' the doors'll lighten it,' he thought, 'an' then it'll be easier to 'andle.'

Off they came (he actually used a

screwdriver this time, although the screws were allowed to bounce around the room and were lost under various items of furniture) and both doors were parked against the sideboard. Now his true genius shone through. Taking the saw, he began cutting the wardrobe in two, vertically of course. The first cut did, unfortunately, remove more of the French-polished veneer from the front, but 'needs must'. Besides, his army experience had taught him that under fire, most initiatives can result in collateral damage, and this one was no exception.

Cutting through the thick top, the saw reached the thin, plywood back of the wardrobe and quickly descended to its base. A final effort brought the saw to the front again as it finally cut through the base. To the experienced eye, the saw-cuts thus produced were not actually straight: in fact they were, frankly, very jagged, which would make the reuniting of the two halves rather tricky, but that test of his craftsmanship in wood would come later.

This is where Terry and Iolo would have come in handy, because the two halves then parted company and fell away from each other, one hitting the floor with a crash, the other striking the sideboard and sliding across one of the doors, making a deep gouge across it.

Thinking about it later, Horatio realised that it would have been better if two people could have held the halves together right up to the very last saw cut, thus avoiding what actually happened. As the two halves said goodbye to each other at the top, they hadn't yet said goodbye to each other at the bottom. But gravity will have its way. They were still both attached to the base, which was struggling now to maintain its integrity against the increasing forces trying to split it apart and release the two halves.

With his saw still working (uselessly) away, he was taken by surprise as the base suddenly split and splintered with a sickening bang and a tearing noise rather like veneer being ripped off. He completely ignored these finer issues and continued to focus on the objective: getting the thing upstairs.

No-one could have anticipated his next move. He stood one of the halves upright and suddenly threw his arms around it, hugging it tenderly but firmly as though in a lover's passionate embrace. In this state of amorous determination, he backed towards the stairs and fell backwards as one foot struck the bottom stair and the half-wardrobe fell on him. But this was part of the plan. In such a supine position, his 'darling' of a half-wardrobe in his arms, he was able to inch up the stairs backwards, one at a time, one buttock at a time and pushing with his feet and turning the sharp bend as he did so, using one buttock against the other in a smooth turn.

His labours took some time and once at the top, the transition from being on his back on the stairs, to being vertical on his feet was not an easy one. At the summit, he realised he was lying on the floor with half a wardrobe pinning him to the linoleum. Like a disenchanted lover he pushed the half-wardrobe off him and rose like a phoenix from beneath it. (Perhaps using the word 'phoenix' is a bit strong, but seeing him pinned beneath what looked like half a coffin brought the idea to mind.)

His efforts were rewarded with success and the girls' bedroom saw for the first time half a wardrobe. And it wasn't too tall either, although there was not enough headroom to stand it up without manoeuvring it so that it stood between the ceiling beams. However, his success was short-lived, as the half-wardrobe was not stable without the other half. It began to twist and threatened to collapse. But he was the master of the situation and placed it face-down (if it could be said to have a face) on the floor awaiting its other half. This too was raised up the stairs in the same lover's embrace, buttock by buttock. (His buttocks were sore for days afterwards giving rise to a rather strange walking gait requiring him to throw one leg out and swing round it before bringing the other into operation.)

Both halves of the wardrobe were eventually reunited, but they were not joined in matrimony. With the help of the girls who temporarily and rather nervously held the two halves together for him, he quickly descended the stairs and from his wonky leaning shed of Pisa brought a hammer, nails and some bits of tomato boxes that had been stored there for many years and were so old they were grey. By nailing these pieces of boxwood across the back, the two halves of the wardrobe were eventually reunited, although they weren't a perfect match and it has to be said that the strips of tomato box looked rather untidy. It was a pity he'd used such long nails, because most of them appeared inside the wardrobe. The ripped and torn base also caused a bit of a problem until he nailed more tomato boxes over the damage pronouncing the object not only desirable but unique. He realised that it possessed certain unusual features, such as rusty nails and torn veneer, but rather than concern him, he persuaded the girls to ignore such details.

'Who's going to look round the back or

inside?' he said, philosophically, one of the girls almost replying to the question, but instinct kicked in and she stopped.

His attempt to reattach the doors required all his ingenuity. Since the two halves never quite mated again, the doors didn't mate properly either. In fact, he had to leave one door off, deciding that modern furniture often had open shelves in it and with some scrap wood (also from the shed) shelves could easily be installed.

One of the girls was heard to whisper: 'If he thinks I'm storing my knickers on dirty tomato boxes as shelves, he's got another thing coming.'

So it was that for the first time the girls had a wardrobe and a wardrobe unlike any other. Sometimes leaders have to overcome practical as well as theoretical difficulties and this time Horatio amply demonstrated his mastery of both. Gladys was too poorly to climb the stairs to look at it immediately. In fact it wasn't until the next day that she was helped upstairs to witness the dark, brooding presence that had been installed in the girls' bedroom, leaning menacingly away from the wall. One of the girls had already tried pushing some folded cardboard under the front to try and persuade it into the vertical but it was just too heavy.

Gladys queried the safety issues on behalf of

the girls (rusty nails sticking out, the strange angle of inclination of the thing and the danger of opening its door) and was assured by Horatio that providing the door was never opened fully, especially when empty, the wardrobe would remain more or less vertical; adding that it was always wise for two people to be present when doing this for safety's sake.

Needing both girls present to open the door was rather annoying, but health and safety considerations are paramount in such things. They did, however, wish their father hadn't nailed a notice on the door instructing the user in how to open the door safely. Being a councillor and an amateur lawyer, he had phrased the notice in legalese that was quite startling. It was some weeks before the girls either tried to open the door, or put anything in it. What they did put in it had to be wrapped in brown paper to ensure it came out without either rust from nails or dust from tomato boxes.

The spare door, meanwhile, was destined for other things as we shall see. 'Waste not want not,' was Horatio's motto as he smiled contentedly at the gift of a wardrobe for the daughters he loved. His confidence had received another boost, unfortunately.

THE FIREPLACE

It is every Welshman's pride to come home to see his family warmed before a glowing fire of Welsh anthracite coal. Indeed, for some years Horatio had been able to satisfy himself on this precise achievement, although the anthracite was somewhat suspect. It wasn't supposed to smoke, but his did. But he still swore it was anthracite. But satisfaction with a domestic fire derives from more than just the coal burning in it; its surroundings, namely the fireplace, contribute too. A drab, utilitarian fireplace detracts from the pride one feels in having such a fire. And so it was that Gladys was occasionally dissatisfied with hers.

The driver of a Volvo Mk IV Waste

Collection and Disposal vehicle is in an enviable position, both physically and economically. From high up in his cab, he surveys at a glance the detritus of others, whilst creating economic opportunities for himself. As Horatio Evans once put it:

'I don't call it rubbish, I calls it gifts.'

So it was, that one Friday morning in November, our keen-eyed 'gift collector' spotted something that shouted out to be saved: an abandoned fireplace.

'Just what she'd like,' he said to himself, 'she' being the frail and strangely unwell Gladys of course.

He repeated his observation to his in-cab partners Iolo and Terry who recognised the potential for getting involved in another dangerous 'project' that their beloved captain of the Mk IV ash cart was plotting. Having experienced, during the wardrobe raid, being able to drive around the streets of Abertump at high speed, leaving enough time to collect such gifts and take them home before the end of their shift, the plucky trio repeated the same high speed tactics. True, as before, much rubbish remained uncollected, but surely a few voters here and there could wait a week for the boys' next round of the town? Especially if the crew made sure that the rubbish of voters in positions of authority was collected as usual.

Like wardrobes, fireplaces are not easy things to handle. They are not only heavy, but if tiled (and they usually are), they are fragile. Ash carts, even the amazing Mk IV are, for some reason, not well designed for lifting or transporting fireplaces, odd-shaped that they are. But the gift this time was in a pretty good position, on open waste ground behind the toilet bowl factory (motto: 'Flushed With Success'). The Mk IV had plenty of space this time in which to manoeuvre. Additionally, the fireplace was leaning almost upright against a wall, beneath some trees. In a flash, Horatio realised he was in luck. Being already upright, it would be a doddle to pass some rope around its middle and hoist it in the air using a branch of one of the trees. Reversing the ash cart beneath the gift once suspended from the branch would provide a straightforward method of loading it onto the vehicle.

Simplicity is the mark of genius. This was simple.

Iolo got some rope and slipped it around the middle of the fireplace. Meanwhile, Terry climbed the tree and was waiting to catch the rope as it was thrown to him. Almost immediately (which was unusual for him), Terry realised that the value of the coefficient of friction between the rope and the branch was too high to allow the fireplace to be hoisted. (Actually, he didn't mention the coefficient of friction, but used a few choice four-letter words that meant the same thing. 'It's stuck' was his considered opinion.) Horatio was not to be beaten. 'Of course it's not going to slip around the branch, idiot! But we'll use some grease so it does,' moaned Horatio, looking skyward.

He nipped back to the Mk IV and brought out another gift, that of a tin of grease that had been hanging around unloved and unwanted outside Will's garage.

The garage was renowned for its highly decorated breakdown lorry that had the owner's philosophy of life emblazoned across its front and sides:

'We have a 23$_{1/2}$ hour breakdown service
(we all needs a break)'
'In God we trust, the rest pays cash'

The grease helped, but it didn't do the whole job. Some lift was obtained, but the rope was still catching on the bark of the tree. 'Teflon's what we need,' shouted Iolo and went to the back of the Horatio Express where he'd noticed a baking tray. 'Bloody ideal, this is,' he boasted, as he bent the tray into a curve to go around the branch to be inserted beneath the greased rope.

'Hey! That's my mam's tray,' cried Terry as he realised what had become of his mother's baking tray, another gift from the voters of Abertump. Horatio was much impressed with Iolo's find. They both heaved on the rope and the fireplace began its ascent. They then hit a snag; they could only lift it about 18 inches at a time with each pull; at that point, they needed to change hands for another pull to raise it a bit more. They made a mess of their first transition from one pull to the next: Iolo let go his grip and Horatio couldn't hold it. So the fireplace dropped to the ground in a cloud of dust with a number of tiles smashed at its base. So Terry was told to 'Get down by yer, goo'boy,' and he slipped to the ground.

Terry's job was to wedge something beneath the gift as it rose each time. How to do this was not obvious to him, or even to a man of normal IQ, but noticing a large pile of bricks across the other side of the waste ground, he busied himself with collecting as many as he could to pile beneath it as it rose, one pull at a time.

The system worked. As Iolo and Horatio hauled on the rope and the gift rose into the air, Terry built up the bricks beneath. The gift was then gently lowered onto them whilst Iolo and

Horatio changed hands and they were ready to haul away again.

Now free-standing bricks, piled one on top of the other are not very stable. Any rough ground on which the first ones are placed won't help either. So quite quickly the two piles began to show a definite deviation from the vertical. In fact, on the fourth lift, the piles were so unstable that Iolo in particular felt distinctly uneasy about the shaky edifice that was rising before him.

'I don't like the look of this bloody thing,' he pointedly grumbled, "Ow 'igh does it have to go before it brains us?' He had a point. The back of the ash cart, the gift's intermediate destination, was at least four feet off the ground. So far, they had managed about two foot six and were worried about losing a couple of toes if the gift crashed to the ground.

It is in just such a situation, when followers are doubting their own abilities and mortal danger seems to threaten, that leaders come into their own. This was no exception. Horatio shouted to Terry to 'Bloody well go and get the cart and reverse it over by yer, quick, while we 'olds it!'

His superior powers of deduction had led him to realise that not all the gift need be at a height of four feet from the ground; if most of it was, then gravity and a good heave would help tilt the rest into the back of the cart, albeit upside down.

The vehicle reversed, although rather too rapidly for comfort, Terry not being used to it. It backed up against the fireplace, pushing it back a little, and sure enough it tilted the top of it into the open jaws of the vehicle.

'Now come by yer with us, you twerp, and 'elp us lift the damn thing into the cart, and don't forget to put the brakes on!' urged Horatio.

(Inspirational words from an inspirational leader.)

Sure enough, it worked. Although the base of the fireplace was only two feet six inches off the ground, the top was higher than the back of the ash cart. The three of them heaved it into the back with relative ease. Tiles flew off the top and front with equal ease, and a crack appeared, running most of the height of it as it struck the steel base of the vehicle. But the major bulk of the thing was intact.

'Don't worry boys, a dab of Polyfilla works wonders! I can always find some spare tiles later to stick on,' assured their leader.

And off they went to 74 Slaughterhouse Terrace to present the gift to the Evans family which was not only blissfully unaware of the impending donation, but one of the girls was taking a bath in front of the fire. Now a Council Mk IV ash cart cannot be kept waiting, especially if it doesn't belong to you. So the girl was turfed out of the tin tub and told to dress in the kitchen 'Whilst me and the boys brings this in.'

Of course Gladys was at a complete loss (again) to understand what on earth Horatio had brought home this time. She was only just beginning to recover from both the wardrobe project and the lean-over construction. Surely he wasn't embarking on yet another 'project'?

'Got something by yer, bach, you'll like. Like new it is. You'll love it. Just rake out the fire will you?'

Gladys was actually pretty sharp, in spite of her mysterious illnesses, but the idea of chucking out one of her daughters from her bath, and scraping out the red hot coals of a living fire onto the hearth, seemed so outside her realm of comprehension that she felt she needed help from the good Lord above, judging by the Welsh prayer she began reciting in a rising, hysterical voice. Totally incapable of executing Horatio's order, she just stood there wide-eyed, whilst he grabbed the poker and pulled out the fire onto the hearth.

Dense smoke rose to the ceiling of the small room, making a thick sulphurous cloud out of which Gladys managed to stagger into the kitchen, coughing alarmingly. (Anthracite shouldn't do this, but this stuff, 'liberated' from the nearest mine did.) If they'd had a canary it would have died instantly. Gas was present at 74 Slaughterhouse Terrace.

Smoke was also rising from the mat in front of the hearth that had received a number of cinders, some of them red hot and was burning nicely. Horatio, steadfast man that he was, simply opened the windows and doors and declared the zone clear, although the front door was still not visible and even the girls couldn't breathe. The motto over the fireplace 'God knows what you're doing' was also totally eclipsed. (Did God *really* know what Horatio was doing, Gladys wondered.)

The next operation was difficult and dangerous. So much so, that both Terry and Iolo escaped quickly once the gift had been successfully unloaded into the room. They had brought the fireplace through the front door alright by man-handling it; but from there onwards it needed careful manipulation in the confines of the small living room. They did this with relative ease, in spite of its weight, by sliding it along the spare wardrobe door and the polished central leaf from the dining table, one that was never used because the room wasn't wide enough.

'See, lads? You needs smooth surfaces to slide things along. Can't beat French polish for that. Just look at that wardrobe door. Marvellous and smooth it is. Just right, you watch,' Horatio assured them.

Perhaps his use of the present tense was misjudged, because the surfaces of both the wardrobe door and the dining table leaf were definitely not smooth by the end of the operation. Deep gouges ran across both polished surfaces.

'Is that more patina, boss?' joked Iolo, smiling.

'Now then, now then, that's enough joking. Sometimes the end justifies the means, boys. Justifies the means. Don't forget that, now.' Philosophy was never absent for long from Horatio's mind. 'Anyway, thanks boys, you can take the lorry back now, see you after the weekend.'

Now the small living room had two fireplaces: one installed, with the remnants of its fire smoking away in the hearth and burning on the mat; and a new one, with quite a number of tiles missing and a crack down the middle, propped up next to it. Without even bothering to remove his coat, Horatio set to.

'No time like the present,' he grunted as he wielded the coal hammer and with a crowbar prised the old fireplace from the wall. Just in time, one of the girls caught the clock as it slid off the mantelpiece, but failed to catch a figurine of Owain Glyndŵr on horseback which fell Owain-first into the pile of burning coal. Everyone was surprised when Owain began to melt and finally burst into flames. The 'solid brass' figurine (another gift) had clearly not been genuine, but that's the risk one takes when picking up gifts from the tip.

It was surprising how easily the old fireplace came away from the wall. So easily in fact, that it was fortunate Horatio was able to throw his hammer and crow bar onto the settee in order to catch the thing as it fell forwards, bringing entire lengths of wallpaper and much of the skirting board with it. A huge effort on his part saw him dragging the old fireplace, pulling at each end in turn, out through the kitchen and letting it fall into a patch of carrots. He'd decided he'd dispense with the wardrobe door and the dining table extension to do this, in order to save time. This wasn't impatience on his part, just showing how focused he was on the objective.

'Anyway,' he argued to himself, 'since I'm chucking this old one out, it don' matter if it gets bashed.'

(That it might bash furniture and fittings in

the process was a trivial and unnecessarily distracting consideration.)

As he demonstrated with the wardrobe, he was not inclined to get confused with detailed measurements and so he hadn't really any idea if the new fireplace would fit. It looked roughly the same size, until he realised that the opening in this new one was definitely smaller than the old one. In fact, the new one was a bedroom fireplace. The fire opening would have to be modified.

Coalhouse hammer in hand, he began sculpting the fire brick bit by bit until it looked about the right size. Unfortunately, fire brick is very fragile and the final knock didn't do it much good. A crack appeared, not where he'd struck it, but right at the back of the firebrick. Investigating the fissure with his crowbar (not the best idea, he admitted afterwards), he mistakenly prised the crack open, wide. To his surprise the crack was still widening of its own accord. Getting onto his knees to see better what was going on, he saw a face staring back at him from within the enlarging fissure. It was Mr Davies his next door neighbour!

Some words, which cannot be printed here, were exchanged through this yawning fissure and more afterwards over the back garden wall. They were to the effect that if Horatio didn't sort out what he'd done, Mr Davies ('The Beast of

Abertump' to his cage-fighting friends) would sort him out.

Cool under fire, Horatio returned to the fire grate. Mixing some stale cement left over from the building of the 'lean-over', adding some fresh Polyfilla for good measure, he sealed the opening in the fire brick. With more heaving and shoving he dragged the new fireplace into place, leaving behind it an interesting set of deep grooves in the linoleum. True, the new fireplace did have an inch gap between it and the wall, but that could be sorted out with a bit more cement later. Luckily for him, he was able to complete the repairs to Mr Davies' fireplace the next day because it was a Saturday and he didn't have to go to work.

'Makes you think you should always start a job on a Friday in case it goes wrong,' he mused.

He spent most of the day sealing the gaps between the new fireplace and the wall and stuffing old rope around the inside of the grate to fill the gap between it and the fire brick. He'd seen this done once and thought it a brilliant idea for filling such gaps. But ordinary rope, such as he used, burns. It is a special heat-proof rope that he must have seen someone using but this difference only became apparent once he'd re-lit the fire. The rope caught fire quite quickly, saturated as it was with creosote. This particular gift had been found behind the watchman's hut at the railway sidings and had been soaked in creosote so as not to rot. People on railways do things like that.

The smell of burning hemp and creosote drifted downwind of number 74 and was picked up at the bus stop in front of Gwen's café. Some customers said they felt unwell from the smell and refused to eat even her renowned Welsh Cakes. Counter-intuitively, Horatio's solution was to close all the doors and windows and to sit it out until the smoking stopped. Unfortunately, this meant that the house was uninhabitable, notably by Gladys who had already caught the bus to her mother's. Once the rope had finished burning (scorching the tiles of the fireplace in the process) it opened up the very gap that it was meant to seal. So what Horatio termed 'natural smoke' (that from the coal) poured into the room.

'I don't mind dirty smoke in its *natural* form,' he told himself as he sat alone, suffocating in the darkened room, 'but I can't abide *unnatural* smoke.'

He had obviously classified the smoke from burning Welsh anthracite as 'natural' and therefore OK. That from creosote-soaked rope was unnatural and not OK. In spite of having entreated the two girls to stay with him, our hero was left alone for some time and was totally invisible under a dense cloud of dark, choking fumes.

'Years ago I swear we used creosote to clear the chest,' he said to himself. 'A couple of hours in by yer might do Gladys the world of good.'

He may have been thinking of coal tar, not creosote. Coal tar was used for the treatment of lice, not a cough. It is actually deadly, as is creosote.

He had to admit that this had not been one of the easiest of enterprises, but wasn't really sure what had been wrong with the plan. His aversion to measuring anything had perhaps been a weakness this time. Hours later, one of the girls ventured back, as much as anything to check that her father was alive. He wasn't there. Frightened, she looked in the back kitchen and into both bedrooms, from one of which she saw him at the top of the garden digging up some late carrots. She went downstairs and into the garden.

She pointed out the foolishness of his enterprise and added a detail about the new fireplace she had noticed: not only was it missing many tiles and had a crack in it, but it was not as wide as the old one so that the old hearth stuck out either side of it. As for the missing wallpaper and wrecked skirting boards, she didn't even bother mentioning them.

The girl did not stay long but returned to her friends, complaining that there was still too much smoke emerging from the gaps in the fireplace. Somewhat dejected, Horatio nipped out surreptitiously and asked one of the Brethren, who was a builder, what he could do about it. He didn't admit he had tried stuffing creosote-soaked rope into the gaps, but felt there must be a solution to the problem that for some reason he hadn't been told about. He came home with a tin of special heat-proof filler that his mate had given him.

'See? Always ask if you're not sure,' he told himself. 'No good pressing on regardless.'

On his way home he noticed in the back lane near Jones' Emporium (Suppliers of Everything Sanitary to the Gentry) a pair of rather interesting items, just standing there, all on their own, alone. They were statues of naked Greek-like goddesses, holding grapes or something; it was difficult to tell exactly what they were holding. They were about four feet tall and were badly broken, one having an arm missing and the other a foot, making the latter look very tense. In both cases their grapes were, strictly speaking, unidentifiable, but the casual observer, given sufficient alcohol and a degree of myopia, might assume they were meant to be holding grapes.

(It was later established that they were holding bags of powdered Polyfilla. They were plaster statues advertising the product. They had been out the back of Jones's shop for years, but rarely on display. Mr Jones's wife felt they were too brazenly naked to be rubbing shoulders, as it were, with customers, especially when young boys would stare at them, rubbing various parts of their anatomy, rather than buying their mother some more paraffin for which they had originally been sent.)

Thus it was that when Gladys returned from her mother's the next day she entered a living room that was transformed. The offending new fireplace was there (leaning outwards); large areas of wallpaper were missing, as were the skirting boards; but at either side of the fireplace, standing on the ends of the old hearth, were two alabaster nudes advertising a new filler cement.

'I can see you like it, bach! No, don't say it, no need to thank me, thank the bloody Council. It was their cart! What a difference, eh?'

The girls said nothing and covered the nudes with tea cloths as soon as their father left for the Buffaloes.

THE KIND KANGAROO

It was a Thursday evening and there he was, our hero, leaning on the end of the bar at The Mad Shepherd chatting to Mavis the barmaid. At least, this is what he thought he was doing. In fact she was never known to engage in a two-way conversation with anyone. She never said a word and kept well away from Horatio, preferring her own company some yards distant.

She wasn't a jolly, buxom maid; in fact she was a thin, rather sad girl, with a pronounced stoop. She looked as though she had just been released from a week in the stocks, her head bowed to avoid missiles. Her head was no longer employed in looking forwards, but downwards. Her hair mirrored her appearance: it too was 'sad', lank, thin and, to be frank, rather greasy. The poor girl could depress anyone just from looking at her. Undertakers lowering into the sacred sod the latest deceased voter of Abertump were hilarious comedians compared with her.

Her dress sense was interesting, consisting of frocks of indeterminate colour and style. They could have been modelled on sacks, hanging from her bony shoulders in the simplest of straight lines. Her habit of always wearing wellies without socks, in summer as well as winter, didn't help either. She never seemed to see the lighter side of life, which was a distinct handicap for a barmaid. As many a visitor discovered, it was no good passing the time of day with her because she appeared deaf to such niceties, as though completely consumed by some secret grief. For her, the end was not nigh: it had arrived. The idea of engaging in a response was anathema to her. Even a customer's smile was wasted effort, because that would require her to look at them, which she never did.

Why Geraint employed her no-one could understand; but the reason was actually very simple: Mavis was so off-putting, so depressing and so uncommunicative that no customer was going to bother complaining to her about anything, especially his watered-down beer.

Geraint didn't want a good barmaid: he needed suicidal Mavis. She was the most effective barrier to customer satisfaction yet devised by man.

But Horatio's caring side was showing that particular evening and he was trying to improve her mood by explaining the finer points of the Communist revolution to come and how she was a downtrodden serf to a capitalist landlord. He pushed home his points by following her up and down the sticky bar, raising his voice against the background chatter and prodding the air in front of her face. Unfortunately, the more she tried to escape the more he slid along the counter, glass in hand, and pursued her. Her depressed mood did not improve and eventually turned to anger.

'Listen, old Geraint might be a right sod, but 'e's never trod on me, never; just let him try! Anyway, why should the likes of you, who always looks as though your face 'as been trodden on tell me what's wrong with my life? I bloody well know what's wrong with my life, thank you, and it's got nothing to do with anyone treading on me. So bugger off.'

This was probably the most she'd ever uttered and brought the pub to a stunned silence. Horatio was surprised that his finger-prodding lecture on the evils of capitalism hadn't done the trick and was about to give up on her when he was tapped on the shoulder by a tall, heavily built man who smiled down on him. (Horatio may have been a big character, but he was barely five feet six.)

'Hello brother, remember me? I'm a Kangaroo,' said the man, offering him a large, spade-sized hand. Now strange things happened at The Mad Shepherd, often involving Horatio himself, but being on the receiving end of this one threw him off balance for an instant.

'You don't remember me, do you?' continued the man, still smiling affably. 'Let me give you a clue: lodge meeting?'

'Oh, bloody 'ell, why didn't you say so?' Horatio replied taking the man's hand and being subjected to some rather strange manipulations of his fingers and wrist, until the stranger's hand disappeared up Horatio's sleeve, leaving him somewhat alarmed.

'Oh, sorry,' he said, 'I shouldn't have done that; I forgot you're only a Calf yet and haven't been initiated into the sacred handshakes of our craft. Habit, I suppose. Sorry.'

'Good God, mun, you scared me then. Is that one of the sacred handshakes then?'

'Yes, it is, but for Heaven's sake don't tell the Great Bison I did it, or he'll have my golden horns removed. I only 'ad 'em two months ago. Anyway, how the Devil are you? Last time I saw you was in the bar of the lodge last week,' remarked the man, resuming a more normal attitude. Horatio began to settle down and glanced automatically at the empty pint glass in front of him. The man spotted the glance and made amends by offering him another pint. He suggested they sit down in a quiet corner somewhere.

Returning from the bar, where Mavis told the stranger, in an exceptional and very rare display of *bonhomie*, to 'Watch out for that bloke, 'e's not right in the 'ead,' thus breaking another record for extended conversation. The man settled down next to Horatio on a bench seat against the wall and sipped his beer, silently.

That Horatio was an aspiring Buffalo has already been made clear. We've seen that he hoped not only to climb the organisational ladder but to perhaps (you never know) benefit from his contact with fellow Buffaloes. Such organisations bring about a natural sense of fellowship and it was this that he enjoyed, as well as the beer. You scratch my back and I'll scratch yours is, after all, very brotherly, even Communist, really.

Whilst the man had been getting the beer, Horatio wondered how to respond to him; for the life of him, he couldn't really remember who he was. If he was a Kangaroo he was a fairly senior

Buffalo and Horatio didn't want to make a mess of this new 'contact'.

The difference between Communist brotherly love and that practised by the Buffs is that the Buffaloes are generally middle-class business people and better off than the Brethren. Asking a favour of a Buffalo could involve something more substantial than would result from asking one of the Brethren. A favour from one of the latter was more likely to be a fag or a pint of beer. A favour from a Buffalo could be much more worthwhile. It should not be thought that only 'posh' people join the Buffaloes. If this were so, Horatio wouldn't be there. And neither would a small handful of other men who earned their living by the sweat of their brows, although some of these were also well off, such as Abertump's farmers. One such man was Eli, the Kangaroo, who was sitting next to him.

He farmed on a small scale and was lucky enough to have one on the floor of the valley where the grass was good and would sustain a dairy herd. So he was actually fairly well off. The two of them said little during their first pint. It was clear that each was sizing up the other. But drinking beer is easy, especially when financed by a well-off Kangaroo. So they got through a reasonable amount of it, Eli introducing himself more fully at last.

That beer loosens the tongue and softens the brain is well known and thus it was that somehow or other Horatio got carried away describing the home he'd made for himself and the DIY projects he'd undertaken, omitting completely any mention of his main occupation as the driver of a Volvo Mark IV ash cart. Perhaps it was because he wanted to demonstrate a common interest, a point of connection, with Eli that he expressed his especial pride in the garden he cultivated. He itemised the crops he grew most years and, it has to be said, exaggerated rather excessively the quantities he produced. Somehow or other, Eli seemed to get the idea that Horatio was a small, struggling market gardener, judging by the sheer quantity and variety of vegetables he claimed to grow. In fact, Eli was amazed at Horatio's claims:

'How that man manages to grow all that stuff in a tiny back garden in Slaughterhouse Terrace is beyond me,' he concluded to himself in a sentiment verging on hero worship.

Horatio had done it again: persuaded someone that he was not only worthy of that person's admiration but deserving of their help. We remember that help came once before from a Buffalo in the shape of a length of copper pipe for his conservatory, so he began to wonder what help might come from Eli, if enough hints were dropped.

Although fellowship is encouraged in the Buffaloes, hierarchy is still respected. For example, a Calf, like Horatio, should think twice about nudging up against the Great Bison in the bar, slapping him on the back and cracking a dirty joke. A strict pecking order is maintained and respected at all times. It was therefore not surprising that Horatio presented our friend Eli with a difficulty, an inversion of their hierarchy in fact. Should a senior member fraternise with a junior one as he was doing?

Whatever the correct protocol, their drinking session inspired in farmer Eli a desire to help Horatio with his horticulture, but he wasn't sure how to broach the idea with him. Specifically, Eli had not long been promoted to the degree of Kangaroo, whereas Horatio was still at the first rung of the ladder, a Calf, which didn't even have a degree. In fact, Horatio wasn't even a Wallaby, a junior Kangaroo, which he hoped to become before long. But eventually Eli broached the subject:

'Look, we're both in the agriculture business and I know how 'ard it can be starting up, so I'd like to help you out. I've got something that'll really bring on your veg: manure. I bet you don't have enough of it to keep that garden of yours in proper shape. Fancy some?'

Horatio was delighted. 'You bet! I don't get much in the way of muck in our place,' he replied, with a chuckle. Gladys may not have wholeheartedly agreed with that statement, because her idea of muck was not her husband's idea of muck. What she called muck, he usually called dust or the natural results of honest labour in the home, brick dust, sawdust, oil, paint splashes, manure from the garden, offcuts of wood, etc.

'That's settled then, I'm glad I can help a fellow agriculturalist. I'll send the boy round with some in a few days' time.'

And so they parted: the Kangaroo pleased with himself at helping out another Buffalo and our Calf delighted to be getting some good stuff from the farm. Horatio left The Mad Shepherd saying to himself with an inner smile:

'Boy, that's bloody great! You watch the veg I'll get next year. Marvellous stuff muck. Can't 'ave enough of it.'

He returned to Slaughterhouse Terrace clearly pleased, which made Gladys worry. 'What was he up to now?' she wondered. She recognised that inner smile, and it meant trouble.

Days went by and nothing untoward

happened. Horatio was constantly in a good mood and, strangely, kept working in the garden almost continually. He had almost dug over the whole plot, which was odd.

'This isn't right; I swear he's up to something,' Gladys repeatedly told herself.

The only clue to what might be happing was not so much the well-dug soil, but an area of cleared, flattened soil in the farthest corner of the veg patch, near the leaning shed of Pisa, as if he was preparing to put something there. But what? Not another shed, surely?

'You're not going to build another bloody monstrosity, are you, I couldn't stand it,' she pleaded.

'Don't you worry, bach, nothing like that. Just you wait and see.'

This oft-repeated phrase 'just you wait and see' was one Gladys heard many times and it filled her with dread. She now knew that he was indeed up to something. It was as though Horatio had said 'Trust me.' It never rang true somehow. Such words never pacified, they terrified.

Two days later, Horatio was bowling down the streets of Abertump with his trusty on-board crew in the Mk IV. He was lucky he was in work and not at home, because unknown to him, at around 11 o'clock, a very large tractor appeared outside number 47, pulling the most enormous trailer piled high with manure. It had stopped outside the wrong house of course, Horatio's being 74. The young lad driving it knocked on the door, which was answered by a shrivelled old man in slippers and a dressing gown.

'Mr Evans? I got a load for you. Where shall I dump it?'

'Nah, I'm not Evans, lad. He's the nutter across the road at 74. This is 47. What d'you mean, a load? A load of what?'

'Manure, mate, manure. This bloke Evans ordered it for 'is business.'

'Well, I bloody well didn't. It's definitely for that nutter in 74.'

'So where shall I dump it then? Can't see a back lane anywhere.'

'If it's manure, just dump it in the front of the 'ouse, that's what I do when I gets a load o' coal.'

'Dressing Gown Man' closed his front door very slowly with the broadest grin he had brought into play for a long while and retired to his front room to watch the fun. The lad climbed back into the tractor, reversed both it and the trailer down the street and up onto the pavement where its load slipped down into the small front 'garden', actually a patch of faded grass and two flower pots. The so-called front gardens in Slaughterhouse Terrace were tiny: no more than three feet in depth, just enough to delineate private property from the public pavement.

Farmers are a funny lot. Being used to driving enormous machines over rough ground, the odd bump here and there is not only ignored, it is not even registered. They also get used to being in natural surroundings and find roads, pavements and even rows of houses unnatural and undeserving of as much care as a town-dweller might consider appropriate. That the load hadn't completely left his trailer was of concern for the lad driving the tractor, because he didn't want to take any back. So he continued to move the tractor and trailer back and fore in order that every bit of muck he'd brought ended up somewhere, even if townsfolk wouldn't think it the best or appropriate place.

Once the front so-called 'garden' at number 74 was full, the only place it could go was the pavement and then the road, although he did try hard to pile the stuff higher and higher in the garden to avoid too much spilling out onto the townsfolk's precious pavements. Satisfied he had done what he was asked to do, he drove off at speed, smoke billowing from the tractor's vertical exhaust and the trailer bouncing joyfully and noisily as though pleased to have been relieved of its distasteful contents.

Its contents were now four feet high in the front garden of the house (covering the lower half of the window) and the rest was spreading like molten lava out into the road where it emitted warm, odour-laden vapours. The pavement, of course, was totally impassable. A Mount Vesuvius of manure lay there, steam rising just like the smoke that slowly drifts from the top of that very volcano. If the smell of burning rope and creosote had previously upset customers in Gwen's café during the fireplace episode, this was far worse.

It so happened that at this moment, the Horatio Express had stopped at the depot for Terry to pick up some spare fags from his locker. The Volvo Mk IV was outside the depot with its engine running, ready to speed off on the rest of its round. Terry seemed to be taking his time for some reason and emerged after several minutes, grinning broadly.

'We've got a change of orders, mates. We've gotta stop the round, pick up a flat-bed lorry and clear up a mess. Some idiot's gone an' dumped tons of crap in the middle of a road! It needs shiftin'. It's all 'ere on this work docket from the boss. Bit of overtime for us tonight,' he sniggered, as he climbed into the cab.

Horatio, drilled into executing emergency orders from his army days, reversed the Mk IV into its bay in the depot yard and jumped into an old flat-bed lorry that was not used much. It took a bit of coaxing to start, but start it did eventually. Terry chucked three shovels into the back of it.

'This 'eap o' junk is only fit for picking up crap from the street,' he commented. 'Where's the job slip, Flash?'

Terry hadn't looked at the sheet, but when Horatio did his foot slipped off the pedal and the old lorry stalled. He was left staring straight ahead, his breathing almost stopped.

'Bloody 'ell, this is *my* place! I know what this is. Oh, God! C'mon, this is serious, boys, it's outside my bloody 'ouse!'

The lorry reluctantly took off, shovels sliding and bouncing about in the back and entered Slaughterhouse Terrace off High Street. The scene was not a pretty one: the town's single policeman (PC Eustace by name, or 'Useless' by nickname) was standing in the middle of the street hoping some traffic would drive down it so he could turn it back. There were few opportunities for Useless to impose his magisterial powers on the people (especially drivers) of Abertump. He was enjoying himself in anticipation of exerting those powers for once.

He had been in the job for years, but he had never fully decided which side of the socio-political fence he was on: was he supposed to be looking after the interests, the peace and the quiet of his fellow voters, or was he supposed to be enforcing the wishes of the faceless ones in political power? He decided that in the end he was an enforcer, a term he liked using. This was the word that had seeped into his subconscious on this occasion.

Neighbours had gathered around the steaming heap, handkerchiefs over noses, discussing how bad things were getting these days with fly-tipping.

'D'you know, I saw an old mattress dumped by the canal last week, which was disgusting, but I never thought someone would fly-tip muck onto our bloody 'ouses!' moaned one depressed woman, whose opinion of her fellow citizens had now plummeted to an all-time low.

Of Gladys there was no sign: either she was incapacitated indoors, or she was out. Luckily for her, she was at her mam's, but her return by the 34 bus wouldn't be long. It would stop outside Gwen's café and an odorous hint of what had been dumped over her front garden may well waft towards her down the wind.

Horatio's lorry drove strangely slowly up to

the offending heap and stopped several yards short of it, as though nervous of the thing. Jumping down from the cab, Horatio imposed his will immediately, by shouting for everyone to clear off so he and the lads could sort things out. That he was particularly fired up by the incident could be measured pretty accurately by the angle at which his hat had been pushed backwards on his head, revealing most of his blanched forehead. This part of his anatomy was rarely seen by the public, being normally reserved for his wife only, and then in the privacy of their bedroom. But it was unmistakeable that the white 'tide mark' caused by the lack of sun on the higher slopes of his forehead was now visible.

Both Iolo and Terry had long learned that when this warning sign could be seen, they shouldn't mess with him: he meant business. They had occasionally discussed this. Iolo, the more mature of the two, reckoned such warning signs were often seen in nature, such as the fur on the neck of a cat rising up when angry. Terry added the example of baboons' bright red bottoms, which showed he hadn't really understood the thing.

Horatio's shouting did not sit well with PC Useless, who was still enjoying the rare exercise of his powers. But when he realised with great pleasure that it was Horatio who would have to sort out this stinking mess and that it was Horatio's own house that had been chosen for this apparent case of gross fly-tipping, he relented somewhat. Both men had clashed before: Useless and Horatio belonging on opposite sides of society, Useless imposing the *status quo* and Horatio trying to wreck it.

'I 'ave to remind you, Mr Hevans, that I am in charge 'ere and if anyone's gonna be told to clear off it'll be me that tells 'em. Anyway, all this muck is valuable hevidence and no-one's to touch it. It's police property now. I gotta collect as much as I can while it's still fresh, as it were!' he chuckled. 'Some idiot's responsible for this fly-tipping, not to mention causin' an obstruction on the highway. I hunderstand that this is your 'ouse? In which case you may be able to sue the perpetrator for compensation, when I do catch 'im that is, and nowt's more certain than that.'

This assertion was interrupted by Dressing Gown Man from number 47 crossing the street, still in his bedroom attire, waving his walking stick.

'Don't wave that at me, it's an offensive weapon, and I'm an officer of the law,' warned Useless.

'Don't be daft, mun, I was going to tell you

who did it, but if you don' wanna know I'll bugger off then,' and he turned to go home.

'Now then, now then, don' be funny with me. If you 'ave hevidence I needs to know. Who was it, then?'

'It was the lad from Eli's farm; 'e done it, I saw 'im.'

This statement stunned Horatio. The good deed from the Kangaroo was about to go pear-shaped and very public, and it already had a bad smell to it. How could he complain about this mess to a fellow Buffalo and a more senior one at that? It was touch and go whether he could maintain an image of firm, reassuring leadership during this crisis as the embarrassment sank in.

At the same time, his eyes noticed just how far up the window of his house the heap was piled. For once, his brain froze and there was a serious danger that his body might freeze too. He realised how awful the situation was but also realised that it wasn't entirely his fault: it was the Kangaroo that had done this, albeit indirectly. His allegiances mixed, he decided that attack was the best form of defence.

'Look, me and the lads 'ave been told to sort this out, so why don' you all let us get on with it. It's only a pile o' crap, after all. We'll soon shift it.'

With which decisive description he jumped

into the lorry, turned it round and began backing it towards the heap, revving loudly so as to show clearly that it was time for onlookers to clear off. His two colleagues had already armed themselves with shovels and were ready for work. He was right: action was needed now, not words.

It hasn't been mentioned previously, but besides considering refuse collecting to be an altruistic social calling (ideal for a communist) he also considered it to be an emergency service. In fact, he had only recently asked his foreman if the telephone number of his house could be advertised in all the town's 'phone boxes, telephone directories and shop windows and officially classed as the fourth emergency service.

'But you 'aven't even got a bloody 'phone!' yelled the foreman with a wide grin on his face, 'is that what you're after, a 'phone?' he queried laughing. 'That's a bloody good one, that is. "Horatio bloody Evans, the fourth emergency service of Abertump!" Hah-hah-hah, hah-hah. Oh that's bloody good that is!'

'The bloody council can install one, can't they? I bet you got one! And I bet you makes private calls on it too,' Horatio asserted, somewhat offended by the foreman laughing at him. Horatio's attempt to get a free 'phone in an attempt to raise his social standing had failed; but clearing up a mountain of manure in an Abertump street certainly gave the argument some weight, Horatio thought to himself.

'After all, what would these silly sods do if we weren't 'ere to rescue 'em?' he told himself. 'We're a bloody emergency service, we are.'

He picked up a shovel ready for action.

'Sorry, but I can't allow you to move this stuff,' declared Useless, 'this is hevidence, I already told you once.'

'So where are you goin' to put all this evidence, then? In your 'elmet? Don't be daft! Listen, do you want this muck shifted or not?' challenged Horatio.

Everyone murmured affirmatively. Useless had been overruled.

'Alright then, shift it, but I need all your names as witnesses,' he declared, opening his little black book, which until that time had rarely seen daylight. After several years in the town he had taken so few notes that his police notebook still only opened at page three. The lads set to. It was slow, smelly work and the stuff was as sticky and as slimy as, well, manure.

'What we needs is a machine,' suggested Iolo, who in spite of his huge size was making slow progress.

Horatio had an idea: 'Carry on lads, while I

go to the pub and use Geraint's 'phone; I know who'll give us an 'and with this.'

Off he went, with a fast, determined step, driven on panic, to 'phone the Kangaroo and ask for help. His call was answered by Eli himself, who soon appeared at the end of the street, driving a tractor with a scoop on the front. No words passed between the two men. They hardly acknowledged each other. The latter realised he'd exaggerated his horticultural needs and the former had been overly generous and overly trusting of his farm hand. The pile on the road and that on the pavement was soon in the lorry, but a significant proportion in Horatio's front garden remained.

'Can't do much about that,' opined Eli. 'Yer gonna 'ave to shift it yerself, mate, by 'and.'

At this point Eli still hadn't got down from the tractor, clearly embarrassed at the misunderstanding that had resulted in this mess. So he turned his vehicle round and zoomed off, muttering to himself that this Buffalo Calf would never make the degree of Wallaby if he carried on like this. Were Horatio's future prospects as a rising Buff now in the balance? Horatio certainly felt so. But the Kangaroo daren't mention any of this to the Great Bison because he too was not innocent. That stupid farmhand of his would be taken down a peg or two when he got back to the farm!

The council lorry took off and dumped the offending material back at Eli's farm, although nothing to this effect was recorded in the depot's records, for fear of tracing the source of the stuff and thereby satisfying Constable Useless's inquisitiveness. There now remained just half a ton of the stuff for Horatio to dispose of. It had always been destined for his back garden and that was where it was going to go.

'Listen lads, we've always 'ad a bloody good laugh together and you're my best mates; so give me an 'and to shift this lot round the back, eh?'

This, thought Terry and Iolo, was asking a bit much. But ash cart crews stick together, like brothers in arms; it's team work. So a deal was struck: Terry would get forty fags and Iolo some new harmonica music.

Iolo didn't live very far, his mother's house where he lodged, being adjacent to the old canal lock, so he brought his own wheelbarrow. Horatio had one too, of a sort. But they needed a third.

Jones' Emporium (Suppliers of All Things Sanitary to the Gentry) always had a pile of them in front of the shop and Horatio managed somehow to persuade him to lend one demonstrate to the council how a Jones wheelbarrow was crucial to successfully tackling the crisis in Slaughterhouse Terrace. If the wheelbarrow passed the test, Horatio promised to promote Jones' Emporium as an official supplier to the Abertump Town Council.

'You'll be listed as "By Appointment", Jonesey.'

Gladys, meanwhile returned. She had passed a pleasant day with her mam, and was in a good mood. For once her chest wasn't too tight and her outlook was almost normal. This changed immediately she saw the mess in her front garden and smelled the smell in her living room. There was no other way to get the stuff from the front of the house to the back garden without wheeling it through the house. Being of a semi-liquid nature, and the route through the house requiring a number of sharp turns with the wheelbarrows, notably around the settee, the stuff had slopped over the edges of the wheelbarrows and was building up on various parts of the floor and furniture.

To be fair, Horatio had taken up the mats, a worthy act, but had done little else to mitigate the manure-covered floor and furniture. The settee seemed to take the worst of it, but the sideboard was also a victim, not of manure, but of wheelbarrow gouges, all at exactly the same height. Gladys turned round in the doorway without saying a word, nipped next door to take a few deep whiffs of Neville's oxygen bottle, and hurried with both girls to catch the number 34 bus again, seeking refuge and renewed solace at her mam's.

This left the lads plenty of leeway to carry on with the task, ignoring the finer points of furniture damage, manure build-up and smell. Thus it was that Horatio's horticultural and Buffalo ambitions took a bit of a bashing; but he wasn't finished yet. Once dumped in the garden, the pile of manure was so enormous that it occupied a good proportion of the entire plot. It had been piled high in the front of the house and therefore didn't look too bad, but once gravity pulled at the unrestrained volume in the back of the house, it spread out.

The relatively modest patch of ground he had cleared in one corner was completely drowned in the stuff. As for the state of his garden overall, it had been devastated by the to-ing and fro-ing of the wheelbarrows. Whilst the carrots, broccoli and potatoes had disappeared under the ever-expanding manure heap, the rest bore the deep furrows of three heavy wheelbarrows and three sets of council-issue boots. At the end of the exercise, Horatio stood proudly in the middle of what was left of his horticultural 'business' with hands on his hips, surveying the smouldering manure heap with pride.

'If that doesn't grow stuff, nothing will,' he thought to himself. Iolo couldn't help but ask Horatio what he was going to do with such a mountainous pile of dung.

'No problem, lad, I'll dig it in. That's the place for muck, in the soil.'

That he was already looking to the future was impressive, a sure sign that his determination and vision were undimmed. There was still no sign of Gladys or the girls and he was secretly glad they weren't there. Although the heap had been moved from the front of the house, liberating their little bit of front garden, he, like many men, hadn't thought of the aesthetics of the result. What had been a small, dried-up patch of grass with a few flowerpots in front of the house, was now a sticky, greenish mess. It had been impossible to scoop up all the stuff and much remained, stuck, as it were in the grass. As for the flowerpots, they had disappeared into shards that had been scooped up with the manure and were buried somewhere in the Vesuvius-like heap out the back. On the walls and window of the front of the house, the high-tide mark of the steaming heap was still clear to see.

These were aesthetic details to Horatio. Unfortunately, they were not details to Gladys, but she was yet to see them. Iolo, the most sensitive of the three did try and point out that they ought to wash down the front of the house, but Horatio, as was his habit, was concentrating on the bigger, strategic issues.

Great leaders tend to do this.

THE HORTICULTURAL ADVENTURE

Now that our hero had such a large pile of manure, the issue occupying his mind was how to incorporate it into the soil of his small garden. For several years he'd nurtured the idea of a using mechanical cultivator on his plot: in fact he had one, albeit missing a minor part, its engine.

He had been given what was the 'business end' of the cultivator by one of Gladys' brothers, Bryn, who was a mechanic with his own small workshop business further up the valley; but he'd kept the engine and thrown out the rest. The blades were intact, if jammed, and the control cables were missing. It was rusty, so that nothing actually moved. But Bryn reckoned that if his daft brother-in-law wanted the thing, he could have it.

'No-one else would be daft enough to try and use it. Without an engine, it's useless,' Bryn reasoned.

'Nothing that can't be fixed,' insisted Horatio. 'I'm not a bloody capitalist sod like you who can afford to buy a new one of these. The proletariat 'ave to make do with what they can get,' he declared to his brother-in-law as he took away the rusty contraption's parts.

Bryn hardly spoke when Horatio was around, in order to save embarrassing his sister, Gladys. It took him a huge effort of will to stay silent. Ever since he'd first met Horatio at Gladys' wedding, he thought his new brother-in-law was a dangerous idiot. He was protective of his younger sister and was often tempted to go down to Abertump and 'sort out that idiot.' We can perhaps understand Bryn's attitude when hearing Horatio call him 'a capitalist sod' at the very moment he was giving Horatio the remains of the mechanical cultivator.

To Horatio this was not meant to give offence. He was merely educating Bryn in the problems of the proletariat. That Bryn might be offended would in any case be seen by any well-indoctrinated Communist as indicative of someone with excessively selfish capitalist interests. People had to be told the truth, Horatio told himself, even if it hurt. Bryn must be shown his misguided ways.

The rusty bits of the cultivator had been stored in Horatio's leaning shed of Pisa for years. Now was the time to bring it out into the full light of day; its moment had come.

It needed an engine and he knew where to get one, round the back of the Abertump Garage. The garage was a peculiar place, built on a steep hillside overlooking Abertump. It had wonderful views of the town; the proprietor, Will Thomas, spending a lot of time appreciating it. He was not, he was the first to admit, a born worker. He was more of a philosopher than a mechanic, reckoning that it was better to take time out and look at the God-given view than work himself to death. There was a poet in him somewhere, in fact, the appreciation of poetry ran in the family.

He was also of a generous nature. His particular brand of philosophy was very benign and based on everyone sharing what he had with others. The Communist Brethren had tried several times to tempt him into the Party but he was an individualist, preferring to develop his own brand of communism, although he never called it that. Basically, he was lazy, his wife maintained, and recklessly generous because he couldn't bring himself to ask customers for payment. You would think that 'forgetting' to ask customers for payment would ensure that the garage was very popular but since it took him ages to do anything, most customers preferred paying someone else in order to enjoy the confidence that their job would actually get done.

'Philosophers have a tough time of it with their wives and customers,' he thought, 'they just don't understand us.'

To add to the picture of Will as a peaceful, philosopher-poet, he smoked a pipe, which was rarely out of his mouth. This in itself was not unusual in those days, but what he smoked in it was. He grew his own tobacco, 'Welsh Gold', on the steep slopes of the coal tip on which his garage was perched. Besides poetry and Welsh hymns this was the one activity to which he dedicated some energy. His father had begun the plantation and devised a method of growing it on the steep slopes. Access was by means of ropes and pulleys attached to a wooden seat, rather like those used by the window cleaners of tall buildings.

The plantation was well disguised, PC Useless being persuaded that it was some special crop with which the Coal Board was experimenting in order to try and green over the pyramids of coal waste. Aided by a plentiful supply of 'muck' it seemed to relish growing on the vertiginous slopes. As a result, Will's garage buildings resembled more closely a tobacco plantation's drying sheds than a mechanical workshop. Of course he had to be careful to whom he sold the stuff and his only customer was Dai Central Eatin', the convener of the trades unions at all seven mines in the valley and nicknamed not because he was a plumber but that he had only two teeth in the front of his head with which to eat.

Will's philosophy of benevolence was a blessing for Horatio, who turned up at the hillside garage humming a Welsh hymn tune, deliberately chosen to endear him to Will. He didn't bother looking for him in the workshop, or down in the service pit; he knew Will'd be looking out over the valley, philosophising and praising Heaven he was Welsh.

'Siwmae, Will?' he enquired.

This familiar form of Welsh greeting was pleasing to Will who was a native Welsh speaker and he replied at length to Horatio's enquiry in his native tongue, confusing him no end. He guessed Will was romancing about the view, because he didn't take his eyes off the horizon, waving his arms about to express his love of the scene and reciting Welsh poetry. Will's father had been a frequent competitor at the National Eisteddfod and was once a runner-up in the poetry prize. Will knew his father's poem by heart. His wife did too, she'd heard it every day for years.

'Will, sorry to interrupt you, bach, but 'ave you still got that old motorbike engine out the back, you know the one, it came off that bike that crashed last year up on the twmp?'

Will didn't take his eyes off the horizon as he acknowledged his visitor: 'Oh, Horatio, what a beautiful day it is and what a day to be Welsh! Oh, Duw, we're so blessed, Horatio, blessed are we that God gave Wales to us,' and he removed his glasses and wiped away the tears from his eyes.

'Aye, Will, s'pose you're right, like. But what about that old engine?'

'Oh, that damned thing, aye, it's still there, rusting out the back. Why? Do you fancy doing it up?'

'Aye, I'd like to 'ave a bash at it. I got a really good use for it and Gladys would be glad if I could 'ave it.'

Using Gladys' name was applying extra emotional leverage to Horatio's request, a softening-up tactic often used by negotiators, he thought. Gladys was very friendly with Will's wife and they both went to the same chapel, Bethesda. Gladys confided in her as the only woman who understood what it was to be married to an idiot. Will, Gladys thought, fell into this category alongside Horatio quite nicely although he caused much less trouble.

'Go on then, pick it up if you want. I don' want it. But it don' work, you know.'

Once Horatio had left, Will turned once more to look at the scene before him and praise the creator of Wales. The Mk IV ash cart drove to the Abertump Garage next day and transported the precious engine to Slaughterhouse Terrace. Horatio's confidence was again at a high point. Although he knew a bit about engines from his army days, it was a long time since he'd stripped one down and done anything serious with it, such as adapting it to power a cultivator for which it was never intended. This was a powerful motorbike engine and totally unsuited to gently turning over the soil. But if he could get this thing going, there were no limits to his horticultural ambitions. Eli the Kangaroo would be impressed and the potential rift between them over the manure affair would be healed.

There was no room to work on the engine in the leaning shed of Pisa, so he had to use whatever flat surface he could find and this was the dining table. Already missing its centre leaf, scored and scarred from the fireplace project, it was looking pretty sad now. The family didn't use it much, except at Christmas and for Horatio doing his pools, so there would be little or no interruption to the family routine (he thought).

Gladys and the girls were still away but were literally on the number 34 bus again returning to Abertump. The bus stopped outside Gwen's café. As they got down, Gladys looked around nervously, wondering if the street had been cleared of the manure and if any crowds were still outside her house. She also sniffed the air to check if anything else had been polluting the town. Relieved that all seemed quiet, she and the girls walked slowly and deliberately down the centre of the street like three cowboys about to clean up the town.

They entered number 74 just as the engine oil was draining into Gladys's washing up bowl, which was filling with foul-smelling, black oil.

'Oh, dear God, what are you doing now?' she pleaded. 'That's my one and only bowl and my one and only dining table! And it still stinks in 'ere!'

This was strong stuff from Gladys; she was normally so passive, saying hardly anything;

Horatio had got used to her silence, but the manure episode must have got to her. She had somehow found the strength to push back at Horatio, something for which he was totally unprepared, especially when endorsed by one of the girls.

'Now look, woman, I got lots o' good muck out the back, and if you'll just be patient, I'm gonna fit this engine to the bloody cultivator, turn over the soil and next year we'll have the best bloody veg and plenty of it. Trust me.'

If only he hadn't used those last two words, he may have got away with it. Gladys and the girls trusted Horatio less than they trusted their local councillors, and he *was* one. But 'trust me' was a sure sign of impending disaster.

'Tell you what, why don' you all go and stay with your sister Doris in Swansea? Nice bit o' sand down by there on the beach.'

'We know there's nice sand there; some of it is sticking your bloody conservatory together,' cried Gladys as she sank onto the settee, from which she stood up suddenly because where she had laid her head on the arm, was a splattering of manure that stank strongly. 'I've only just come back from Mam's, now you're chucking us out again! I spend more time on that bloody 34 bus than in my own 'ome.'

For some reason, probably known only to chemists, the smell of manure seems to linger, even when washed out with bleach, which is what Terry had done to the settee. It certainly brightened up the back of it, which was now almost cream (in patches), quite a different colour from the rest, which was brown. Perhaps the muck had soaked into cracks in the linoleum: Horatio wasn't sure, but Gladys and the girls reckoned the place smelled worse than a cow shed. As any farmer will tell you, if you're working with muck all day, you don't notice the smell, eventually. This is probably the stage that Horatio and his two colleagues had reached: they had developed an olfactory immunity to it.

It was not, however, an immunity shared by Gladys and the girls. They didn't spend more than five minutes in the room before all three of them went upstairs, packed two suitcases again and caught the next bus to Swansea. Horatio, ever the generous head of the household, gave them the bus fare. He agreed that Gladys did spend more time on a bus than in the house.

'Best the girls clear off. At least it'll give me some time to sort out this little baby,' he said, grinning and rubbing his hands. 'She'll feel better when this is done and the garden's tidy again. Women just don't understand these things.'

We shan't go into the details involved in the dismantling of the engine, the battle he had with rust (solved by immersing it in a tin bath full of petrol, which raised safety questions all its own) or the fact that once reassembled, it presented Horatio with significant problems as to how to attach it to the remnant of the mechanical cultivator he had in his shed. Suffice it to say, that with extremely reluctant help from his brother-in-law, Bryn, he managed to have it welded to the rusty remains of the cultivator and all was ready for commissioning. How Bryn kept his temper during this work was, even to him, a total mystery. Having Horatio breathing down his neck during the operation was almost intolerable, especially when his welding work was criticised. Bryn felt like welding Horatio to the thing!

The commissioning of the horticultural wonder-machine took place, unfortunately, on a Sunday. Bearing in mind that Sunday in Wales was then a hallowed and essentially silent day, the roar of an engine was frowned upon by the voters of Abertump. To a secular Communist like Horatio, this seemed nonsense and rather than deterring him from making a noise, he saw it as his duty to make more.

Gladys, eventually returned from Swansea and beginning to feel she could stay in her house a bit longer this time, was distressed at this attitude. She expressed her shame to her sister-in-law as they made their way to the Bethesda Chapel that morning. It was an event to which she looked forward each week, not only to make her peace with her Maker, but for the fellowship it provided. In fact, it was pretty well the only occasion when she could feel at ease, because she was doing something just for herself and which she enjoyed. It was also an occasion when she felt safe; the old chapel provided a safe haven, both physically and emotionally. It was neutral territory, never to be spoiled by Horatio and his secular theories. In logistical terms it was also easy to get to: Bethesda was in the next street.

Sitting in her allotted pew alongside her sister-in-law that morning, both of them resplendent in feathered hats, Gladys couldn't help feeling, in spite of her liberal use of perfume, that she was not smelling her freshest, somehow. The smell of manure seemed to have clung to her clothes; or perhaps her nose just couldn't rid itself of the lingering molecules of the stuff. She enjoyed singing the first hymn, 'Hapus Wyf I' (Happy am I), to a favourite hymn tune of hers, although she hated the words with a vengeance. The hymn over, as they sat down, the organ winding down with a solemn drone, the visiting preacher, the Rev Goronwy Roberts stood up in the pulpit and stared out threateningly at the congregation.

Gladys suddenly had a fleeting and un-Christian realisation that the preacher was from Llanelli, the town from whence came all her grief and sadness; the very town that was responsible for the birth of Horatio ap Llewelyn Evans. She tried to put the thought to one side and 'think Christian'. But it was difficult.

'He even haunts me in chapel,' she commented to herself.

But in spite of making a determined Christian effort not to think about it, Llanelli was not to be ignored. Somewhere not far away, someone had started up an engine that was making the most infernal noise. Defying many attempts to start it, the engine on the horticultural wonder-machine had at last spluttered deafeningly into life and was pouring out smoke like a North Atlantic destroyer laying a wartime smoke screen.

'Oh, good God, help us!' she inwardly groaned, 'I know what that noise is and I know exactly where it's coming from. He's started that engine of his.'

The preacher didn't employ a loud voice, at least initially. He was one of the theatrical Welsh preachers who always began quietly and slowly, beguiling and coaxing his congregation with a seductive mix of empathy for them and admissions that he too was a sinner. He would follow this gentle, forgiving seduction by a gradual crescendo of condemnation for their sins, before finally damning his entire congregation to eternal Hellfire if they weren't more Christian during the coming week. If his blood pressure held out, he would thump the pulpit and punch the air to add emphasis to his curse that he cast upon the wicked sinners before him.

Whatever one's spiritual inclinations, such orators never fail to give congregations a good emotional ride. The pleasant feelings congregations feel when exiting a chapel may have been as much due to the emotional relief that came after experiencing such a roller-coaster as in surviving the damnations of Hell itself. But this time the preacher's strategy was not working. The noise of the spluttering 500 cc engine as it powered the cultivator was winning the competition for the congregation's ears. It was also winning the congregation's noses, because the chapel must have been downwind of the garden at nearby 74 Slaughterhouse Terrace and was being treated to a good dose of unburned petrol fumes and exhaust gases.

As the preacher steadily increased his volume to match the competition from the cultivator, looking less confident by the minute, the congregation became restive, Gladys being the most unsettled of all, receiving puritanical looks from several quarters, not least of all from her adjacent sister-in-law. Gladys decided to leave. As she did so, she could swear the preacher's words were meant just for her:

'Damned are those who do not keep the Sabbath to keep it holy. Damned saith the Lord. Damned I say!'

'Alright, I got the message,' she thought to herself as she felt the glare of condemnation from both preacher and congregation and stumbled, blushing deeply, out the door.

Entering Slaughterhouse Terrace, she ran the gauntlet of numerous neighbours who were standing on their doorsteps discussing the awful disturbance and the clouds of smoke coming from number 74. They were mostly women, whose body language said much. They had all folded their arms under their breasts and their chins had been tucked in, the effect being a communal attempt at silent condemnation. They adopted this judgemental stance in pairs of adjacent doorways. They were a guard of shame past which Gladys had to scurry.

The men, although fewer, were mostly laughing and had gathered in a group in the centre of the street outside the house. Dressing Gown Man from 47 was with them, still in his pyjamas, waving his stick and shouting comments about 'that nutter in 74'.

This was not the sort of quiet Sunday morning Gladys wanted or deserved. Her nerves were in a terrible state and repeated journeys on the number 34 bus hadn't helped. She needed rest. Not knowing whether to smile shyly at her female judges or to try and complete her walk without looking to left or right, she at last made it to the front door, which was wide open, exhaust fumes drifting out into the street.

In the garden, the Battle of the Somme had been faithfully reproduced. The machine, being equipped now with an engine twenty-five times as powerful as the one with which it was born, was churning up everything into which it came into contact. Any vegetables that had survived the wheelbarrows and council boots were in shreds; deep trenches had been created across the garden in a strangely random way. The reason was simple: it was out of control.

The powerful machine was doing its stuff, but it was too powerful to handle. Horatio was committed to hanging on as best he could as it ploughed its way across the plot, only changing direction when it hit something, at which point it dug itself in, deeper and deeper until it hit a large stone or other substantial subterranean obstacle. The topology thus created was amazing. Hills and valleys, some quite deep had been created everywhere. One particular trench, the most impressive and the most reminiscent of the Somme, was about two feet deep and extended several yards towards the leaning shed of Pisa, but had luckily missed it. Instead, it had continued onwards until it hit the foundations of the neighbour's wall; at which point it dived ever deeper, which was precisely the clever mechanism that Barnes Wallis employed for destroying damns in Germany.

The manure heap, meanwhile, remained in solemn control of its corner of the garden. None of it had moved or been moved. Now the mound was just another mound amongst many and it didn't stand out quite as much, although it was still smouldering threateningly. As for Horatio, if you didn't know him, the look on his face seemed to indicate that he was enjoying himself. But to a seasoned observer, his face showed he was terrified.

He had an otherworldly, fixed grin on his face, as though lockjaw had set in. His eyes, whilst staring into the distance as though shell-shocked, had within them a look of pitiful appeal, begging for help. The poor man was now the tortured victim of the terrifying machine, condemned never to let go, yet unable to stop it. The pieces of string he had used to replace the missing steel control cables had let him down. The 'thing' was now a monster, destined to patrol the garden forever, creating havoc and destruction wherever it went. Horatio had become the Flying Dutchman of the horticultural world.

As the cultivator continued to drag him along behind it, showing no mercy, it was making a return journey from the other end of the garden at a depth of about two feet, when it suddenly struck a stone and veered towards the leaning shed of Pisa. The machine, not meeting any substantial obstacles, subterranean or otherwise, literally burrowed its way beneath the shed which seemed to explode in a cloud of matchsticks and dust. It was in ruins, having spilled out its entire contents (mainly tomato boxes) across the garden. His liberated British Railways shovel was the only item recognisable, lying in the one corner of the edifice that remained.

With a loud bang and much smoke, the fiendish contraption itself then stopped when it was three feet down. The monster had overdone it. The crankshaft was broken and, having had its final fling, had ground to a halt. The hole it was digging then began filling with water which appeared to be fizzing like pop in a bottle. It had first struck a water pipe and then the gas main. It was at this moment that Gladys appeared, smoking her habitual Woodbine. Suffice it to say the explosion was fairly loud and she was thrown backwards onto the manure heap unhurt but shocked. Her fag was nowhere to be seen.

The ignited gas produced a rather beautiful flame that was quite impressive. Luckily, the machine had not severed the gas main completely and the water and soil were partially blocking the break. The fire brigade did a splendid job and gas supplies were restored by late evening. Horatio was disappointed, but at least the terror of the experience was over. All that work on the engine and all he had to show for it was a wrecked garden, no vegetables, no shed, and a gas flame thirty feet high. Not to mention his reputation with his neighbours that had now hit a new low. Mr Davies the cage-fighter next door had to be restrained by his wife and two men from 'fixing that bloke once and for all.'

'If there's one thing I've learned, boys,' he admitted in The Mad Shepherd next day, 'don't be taken in by a Kangaroo.'

His listeners now realised how far gone he really was.

NO SURRENDER

We began Horatio's story in Llanelli, where he was born. In spite of the quarrels, his parents Arthur and Lavender Evans maintained their peculiar relationship faithfully: Arthur stuck at it because he believed he had no alternative; Lavender because in spite of all the years that had passed, her sense of revenge had still not been satisfied. Her parents, throughout this period, had steadfastly refused to contact her. The stories they were compelled to tell their friends and the rest of the family in order to perpetuate the lie that she was living in New Zealand, became ever more complex as a result.

They didn't go as far as forging false letters from Lavender (although they once bought some used New Zealand stamps) but the yarns about her allegedly successful life in the antipodes with a brain surgeon, had to be kept fresh and interesting. To do this, both of them had to constantly consult each other to rehearse the stories in order to ensure they didn't lay a trap for the other with conflicting 'facts'. This constant strain on them may have led to Lavender's father deciding he'd had enough of the florist business and was going to sell up. It had been a good business and the generous price he got for it surprised him. They decided it would be best if they retired and moved away from the rest of the family in Bristol, thus relieving them of the need for constant story-telling.

They moved into a pleasant, but rather modest bungalow, in Weston-super-Mare. They had decided to downsize, having had enough of keeping both a shop and a four-bedroomed house in Clifton. The bungalow was a clone of many similar ones in the street behind the sea front: painted white, it had a small front garden, a garage and a reasonably-sized back garden which would keep them quietly busy. The net financial result of this change was that they had quite a bit of spare cash. Several months passed and they both agreed that retirement was good. It was as they were walking along the promenade one day that Lavender's mother looked across the Severn

Estuary to South Wales and remarked:

'It's strange to think that somewhere over there is our daughter and our grandson. I am beginning to feel bad about not being in touch. Do you think we ought to do something about it?'

This came out of the blue; she even surprised herself by mentioning it. Perhaps now that they were both comfortable, and living away from friends and relatives, they had subconsciously reassessed their relationship with their daughter. Since they hadn't seen their grandson Horatio at all, except in some early photographs, their instinct for nurturing their offspring may have suddenly awakened.

So it was that Lavender received a surprise letter from her mother. Perhaps 'surprise' is too mild a word: she had almost forgotten she had parents at all. Their suggestion that they not only visit her but also their grandson, Horatio, seemed unimaginable. Besides the unexpected element of receiving such a missive, the implications immediately washed over her like a tidal wave. To show them the meagre Llanelli house where she lived and the extremely strange house where their son lived was something she couldn't imagine happening without significant planning, if it were to happen at all. What on earth would her parents think?

It gave rise to a unique occasion: she asked Arthur to sit down with her and discuss something, a request he found distinctly unnerving. Brain-to-brain contact between them had long been sporadic, to say the least. Suffice it to say that once the idea had been spoken of out loud, and a few days had passed, Lavender realised she had unknowingly missed her parents. And so she spoke in favour of seeing them again. That they should then go on to meet Horatio was, however, another matter. Arthur and Lavender had visited him only three weeks previously, after the lean-over had been completed, and both had beaten a hasty retreat to Llanelli.

They hadn't seen anything like it before. Arthur was convinced his son was nuts, whereas Lavender was convinced they had let him down; that if Horatio's wife, Gladys and her family, had been more supportive his true talents would have come to the fore and his life in Abertump would have been so different. Eventually, letters were exchanged between Lavender and her parents and a date set for them to visit. Not having a spare room in Tinplate Terrace (Lavender alleged) her parents readily agreed it would be no inconvenience for them to stay at an hotel.

The visit sent Lavender into a spin. The house had to be cleaned from top to bottom and several DIY jobs that Arthur had been avoiding for years had to be completed. In spite of hitting the targets she'd set for improving the house, she realised that there were two things that she could never improve: her neighbours and the neighbourhood. One plan she hatched was to meet her parents on neutral territory, but Arthur wouldn't hear of it.

'There's nothing wrong with this place,' he insisted, 'if they're too stuck up to see where we lives they needn't come.'

Lavender's years of revenge had made its mark; kindly co-operation between the two of them was going to be difficult, especially for Arthur. But he hit on a plan of his own which pleased Lavender no end: he would spend a couple of days 'on holiday' in the shunting yard sheds where years ago he had found a warm place to lay his head and some friendly male companionship. That way, Lavender could weave whatever stories she liked about him and he would be away from the tension and artificiality that the visit was bound to generate.

As for her parents, seeing their genius grandchild, for that is how she described her son Horatio, was another matter. They had written to him and received a short reply on a scrap of paper to the effect that if his grandparents wanted to visit 74 Slaughterhouse Terrace, they were welcome provided they took him and his family as they found them.

'They can come 'ere if they want to, even if it's taken 'em long enough to think about it,' he declared to Gladys, who, like Lavender, was dreading the experience.

The day of the visit arrived. Lavender's parents turned up in their large, green Rover one Tuesday at around midday. The car was enough to signal to the neighbours that something of note was happening. Rather than enhance Lavender's status, however, it diminished it.

'Told you she was stuck up,' the neighbours agreed with each other.

Entering the house, her parents' behaviour was stiff and circumspect. Two pairs of English middle-class eyes scanned every corner, registering the quality of the ornaments, the carpets, pictures (of which there was only one, a reproduction of a view of the tinplate works at night) and finally, the incomplete set of crockery and miscellaneous cutlery set out on the chintz-covered table (a strategically placed plate covering a deep stain). We can imagine how difficult the conversation became once polite 'hellos' had been exchanged. It had been decades since they had seen each other or even spoken.

Lavender's mother was the first to break the ice and pleasantly surprised her daughter by apologising for the way they had abandoned her after the birth of Horatio. Lavender was shocked but secretly pleased; up until that moment, she had been a lonely exile living in a foreign land; now she had before her two other 'normal', English people who could perhaps understand her feelings and even support her.

Lavender made excuses for Arthur having to work overtime and not being there. As though to smooth over his absence, she stressed what a good man he was and how appreciative she was of his substantial earning capacity. (She later wondered how she had managed to say these things about the husband she called a Welsh twerp.) Tea was served and drunk. Victoria sponge was consumed, notably by her father, and eventually the atmosphere relaxed.

Then, out of the blue, they announced to Lavender the news they had agreed on: they had lots of spare cash from the sale of the business and would like Lavender to have some. They also wanted to give some to their grandson, Horatio. This softened the atmosphere immediately. Here, Lavender realised, could be her chance to rise out of the scruffy backwardness of Tinplate Terrace and seek a house in the tree-lined uplands of

Llanelli's more desirable districts amongst people who knew what natural spaghetti was. Lavender, in spite of all the years of anger, revenge and sadness, suddenly lit up with optimism. But what was the catch? They said they also wanted Horatio to have some money.

Lavender and Arthur had had little to do with him since his marriage, Arthur saying that his son ought to be left alone to 'plough his own furrow'. In private, Arthur thought his son needed psychiatric care and would rather keep his distance from 'the nutter at number 74', as Horatio's neighbour Dressing Gown Man called him. As for Horatio's political activities, Arthur was genuinely worried; to him, anyone dabbling in such things was bound to be either nuts or devious or both.

Lavender's parents stayed for almost two hours and left for their hotel at around 4 pm. Their departure was witnessed by numerous housewives who suddenly and simultaneously found some work to do on their doorsteps. As the Rover pulled away from the kerb and she waved her parents goodbye, Lavender was able to smile at them for the first time for a long time.

'Now we'll see who has the last laugh,' she smiled to herself with warm satisfaction.

Her parents' plan was to visit Horatio the

following morning at Abertump. They hadn't been to the small mining town before and were not looking forward to it. The idea of visiting a dirty industrial area did not attract them after living in the clean, whitewashed coastal resort of ozone-washed Weston-super-Mare. In fact, when they got to their room at the hotel and closed their bedroom door, they were initially both silent about their impression of Tinplate Terrace and their forthcoming visit to a mining town.

'Not much of a place, is it?' her father said, cautiously.

'I know, I think it's just awful. All those dirty, tiny houses and probably dirty tiny people in them too,' whispered her mother, in case anyone heard her. This was epiphany time.

Neither parent wanted to say what they really felt about Lavender's standard of living, except that something must be done to rescue her.

'She *is* our daughter, after all is said and done. There's been lots of water under the bridge; she's made her bed and has been lying in it. She mustn't count her chickens before they hatch, but blood is thicker than water.'

Scattering these aphorisms into the air was a euphemistic way of saying what neither of them wanted to say: they'd left their daughter in a mess all these years and they owed her something.

As for Horatio and his potential windfall, that was to be another thing altogether, although as yet he knew nothing about it. Proud, independent and somewhat Bolshie, the thought of him accepting a gift from bourgeois grandparents who'd never bothered with him before was an impossibility, philosophically and politically (notably the latter). Having money and, by definition, becoming a capitalist, would totally ruin his standing with the Brethren, a reputation that had built up over many years, although it would improve his standing with the Buffaloes.

But the manure episode with the Kangaroo was beginning to set his mind against the Buffaloes. His ascent to the degree of Wallaby had not yet happened, although it was promised to be soon, and he was feeling a little let down. As a result, he decided to specialise, for the time being, *mostly* in Communism and its close cousin Trade Unionism and nurture the Brethren's support. As an *addendum* to this confused non-decision, he told himself that if, on the other hand, any useful opportunities came from being a Wallaby he would still remain a Buffalo. To Horatio this (unaccountably) seemed to clear the air. He was to be a Communist first with Buffalo leanings. Which, really, is what he already was.

Leaders' minds work in ways unfathomable to ordinary folk. One characteristic of leaders is their ability to cope with uncertainty. In this case, however, Horatio's views were not only uncertain but polar opposites. Nevertheless he saw nothing wrong in being both a Buffalo and a Communist, or, as he had now decided, a Communist and a Buffalo. Which position, we may observe, is precisely what he had been all along. Genius is difficult to understand sometimes.

'We'll get that bloody red flag flying over Abertump yet,' he decided, 'and if anything comes of the Buffs, I'm their man.'

To cut a long and painful story short, his grandparents' visit to 74 Slaughterhouse Terrace was not a success. One look at the place ensured that they were not only shocked but unable to comprehend what Horatio had been up to. Before they entered the house, they noticed the high-tide mark of the manure heap on the front window and walls and could smell the ground was still saturated with the stuff. A tour of the cottage revealed the strange, leaning wardrobe with the door missing in the girls' room; the smoking, cracked fireplace surrounded by torn wallpaper, missing skirting boards and two large, naked, plaster statues holding sculpted samples of Polyfilla.

As for the conservatory or lean-over, Horatio's grandfather jumped back into the living room as soon as he entered it, fearing for his life in case the thing collapsed. (The girls' three lengths of wood were still supporting 'Jesus Walking on the Waters'.)

He did, however, cautiously poke his head around the door a second time to fully appreciate the bath arrangement with its long copper pipe, ending in a fine collection of brass 'adaptions'. But it was the sight of the 'garden' that made him go pale. As his eyesight penetrated the distorting panes of mixed glass in miscellaneous scrap windows, he saw the Battle of the Somme in miniature. This was something he had never seen before, even in photographs. In a corner, the manure heap sat like Vesuvius, steaming menacingly, the vapour drifting slowly across the trenches as though they had just been shelled.

The remains of the leaning shed of Pisa were still scattered across the garden. The deep trenches and (he assumed, shell-craters) held his attention as though he had been drugged.

'What am I looking at?' he wondered. 'How on earth could this have happened; it's as though the place has been bombed. Look at those trenches and the shell holes! Is it meant to be a model of a battlefield?'

The man was clearly bewildered. Horatio noticed his grandfather's face had fixed itself into a stare, his mouth open in a fixed rictus of shock as he gave his own, rather full description of what had happened.

'What on earth is this grandson of mine on about?' he wondered. 'The man is mad! He doesn't need money to fix things, he needs treatment!'

The grandparents felt sorry for Gladys who was unable to get a word in edgeways. It was clear the stress had taken its toll on her: she just wanted a fag and a lie down. Perhaps the final straw that decided the grandparents to back out of the house quickly was Horatio's diatribe on the latest communist thinking followed by the rather badly timed statement, spoken clearly and with some conviction:

'I'm going to be a Wallaby next month.'

That did it! That he was certifiable was now clear. The best plan was to drive away and find a café somewhere where they could calm their nerves and have a cup of sweet restorative tea. The Rover was a powerful car, which showed, as it sped off in a cloud of smoke that it had never produced before, its accelerator being pushed to the floor for the very first time. The end of the street was reached in seconds and the car disappeared round the corner, never to be seen again.

Gladys looked at Horatio with a blank stare, unable to believe he'd just looked such a potential gift horse in the mouth, refusing a significant cash gift from his grandparents. She now realised she was destined to continue to live amongst Horatio's house-improvement schemes for many years.

A Woodbine was lit and her asthma pump used on the 'high' setting. Meanwhile, six months later, Lavender, Horatio's mother, had found a nice house in the foothills of Llanelli, away from the railway sidings and the tinplate works. Arthur was reluctantly happy with his new surroundings: he'd not had to do a thing to get so nicely set up. He even began to feel a little soft on Lavender; she wasn't such a bad catch after all.

***

TO BE CONTINUED...

Printed in Great Britain
by Amazon